T0114433

Life à la Henri by Henri Charpentier and Boyden Sparkes

Clémentine in the Kitchen by Samuel Chamberlain

Perfection Salad: Women and Cooking at the Turn of the Century by Laura Shapiro

Cooking with Pomiane by Edouard de Pomiane

High Bonnet: A Novel of Epicurean Adventures by Idwal Jones

Katish: Our Russian Cook by Wanda L. Frolov

The Supper of the Lamb: A Culinary Reflection by Robert Farrar Capon

THE PASSIONATE EPICURE

MARCEL ROUFF

THE PASSIONATE EPICURE

La Vie et la Passion de
Dodin-Bouffant, Gourmet

Translated by Claude

RUTH REICHL

SERIES EDITOR

Illustrated by Charles Mozley
Preface by Lawrence Durrell
Introduction by Jeffrey Steingarten

THE MODERN LIBRARY

NEW YORK

Introduction to the Modern Library Food Series

Ruth Reichl

My parents thought food was boring. This may explain why I began collecting cookbooks when I was very young. But although rebellion initially inspired my collection, economics and my mother's passion fueled it.

My mother was one of those people who found bargains irresistible. This meant she came screeching to a halt whenever she saw a tag sale, flea market, or secondhand store. While she scoured the tables, ever optimistic about finding a Steuben vase with only a small scratch, an overlooked piece of sterling, or even a lost Vermeer, I went off to inspect the cookbooks. In those days nobody was much interested in old cookbooks and you could get just about anything for a dime.

I bought piles of them and brought them home to pore over wonderful old pictures and read elaborate descriptions of dishes I could only imagine. I spent hours with my cookbooks, liking the taste of the words in my mouth as I lovingly repeated the names of exotic sauces: soubise, Mornay, dugléré. These things were never seen around our house.

As my collection grew, my parents became increasingly baffled. "Half of those cookbooks you find so compelling," my mother complained, "are absolutely useless. The recipes are so old you couldn't possibly use them."

How could I make her understand? I was not just reading recipes. To me, the books were filled with ghosts. History books left me cold, but I had only to open an old cookbook to find myself standing in some other place or time. "Listen to this," I said, opening an old tome with suggestions for dinner on a hot summer evening. I read the first recipe, an appetizer made of lemon gelatin poured into a banana skin filled with little banana balls. " 'When opened, the banana looks like a mammoth yellow pea pod,' " I concluded triumphantly. "Can you imagine a world in which that sounds like a good idea?" I could. I could put myself in the dining room with its fussy papered walls and hot air. I could see the maid carrying in this masterpiece, hear the exclamations of pleasure from the tightly corseted woman of the house.

But the magic didn't work for Mom; to her this particular doorway to history was closed. So I tried again, choosing something more exotic. "Listen to this," I said, and began reading. " 'Wild strawberries were at their peak in the adjacent forests at this particular moment, and we bought baskets of them promiscuously from the picturesque old denizens of the woods who picked them in the early dawn and hawked them from door to door.... The pastry was hot and crisp and the whole thing was permeated with a mysterious perfume.... Accompanied by a cool Vouvray,...these wild strawberry tarts brought an indescribable sense of wellbeing....' "

"Anything?" I asked. She shook her head.

Once I tried reading a passage from my very favorite old cookbook, a memoir by a famous chef who was raised in a small village in the south of France. In this story he recalls being sent to the butcher when he was a small boy. As I read I was transported to Provence at the end of the nineteenth century. I could see the village with its small stone houses and muddy streets. I could count the loaves of bread lined up at the *boulangerie* and watch the old men hunched over glasses of red wine at the café. I was right there in the kitchen as the boy handed the carefully wrapped morsel of meat to his mother, and I watched her put it into the pot hanging in the big fireplace. It sizzled; it was so real to me that I could actually smell the daube. My mother could not.

But then she was equally baffled by my passion for markets. I could stand for hours in the grocery store watching what people piled into their carts. "I can look through the food," I tried to explain. "Just by paying attention to what people buy you can tell an awful lot about them." I would stand there, pointing out who was having hard times, who was religious, who lived alone. None of this interested my mother very much, but I found it fascinating.

In time, I came to understand that for people who really love it, food is a lens through which to view the world. For us, the way that people cook and eat, how they set their tables, and the utensils that they use all tell a story. If you choose to pay attention, cooking is an important cultural artifact, an expression of time, place, and personality.

I know hundreds of great cookbooks that deserve to be rescued from oblivion, but the ones I have chosen for the Modern Library Food Series are all very special, for they each offer more than recipes. You can certainly cook from these books, but you can also read through the recipes to the lives behind them. These are books for cooks and armchair cooks, for historians, for people who believe that what people eat—and why—is important.

INTRODUCTION

Jeffrey Steingarten

This delightful little classic was probably the first gastronomic novel ever written, printed in a tiny edition in 1920, then properly published in 1924. The charming translation by "Claude" is the only one into English. It was first published in London in 1961 and a year later in New York City, and has been out of print for a generation. We are very lucky to have it back.

Our hero, Monsieur Dodin-Bouffant, is a distinguished jurist, now retired and living with one servant in a small, comfortable house in his ancestral town. He has dedicated his life, every waking hour, to the refinements of cuisine, which is to say French cuisine—eating and cooking, thinking and talking about it. Though word of Dodin's gastronomic genius has spread throughout the world, he remains "unpretentious, kindly, simple; devoting with ever more conscientious gravity and more concentrated ardour, the powers and meditations of his riper years to the subtle and magnificent art to which he considered he owed, for the traditional glory of his country, the best of himself and the whole of his active genius." For Marcel Rouff, Dodin's creator, eating is an art, an act of patriotism, and much more.

Dodin-Bouffant (we never learn his given name) is surely the most famous character in gastronomic fiction. He is pleased, though perhaps not completely surprised, when the Crown Prince of Eurasia, vacationing in the Jura to take the waters, invites him to dinner. The Prince's motive is both to display his own epicurean abilities and to win a return invitation to Dodin-Bouffant's table. These dueling dinners are the central event of the book, the scenes with which *The Passionate Epicure* is always identified in France. One passage, a page or two, right in the middle of one of the dinners is surely the most quoted. Why should this be? There are, after all, a multitude of wonderfully mouthwatering eating scenes throughout the book; they draw us from beginning to end like a truffle tied to a pole, even when the plot itself slackens. The book brims over with nice apothegms and culinary word-paintings both sensitive and vivid. And for sheer suspense, satire, and sensual satisfaction, we would surely turn to the scene of Dodin-Bouffant's covert meeting, toward the end of the book, with a beautiful, young, rich, blond female worshiper who, on top of everything else, proves to be an even greater gastronomic genius than he. Then why the two dinners with the Prince of Eurasia? The reason is simple. The reason is *pot-au-feu.*

For the French, *La Vie et la Passion de Dodin-Bouffant, Gourmet* is about the *pot-au-feu* Dodin serves the Prince—a common and simple dish, but for centuries very close to the soul of France, the foundation of empires, it has been called. Perhaps that is why several epicurean friends in Paris assigned this book to me ten years ago as required reading. My command of French, once sufficient to subdue Corneille and Racine, had by then become a blunt, corroded tool, and so I limited myself to the famous Chapter 4. And there it was—not only the most inspired description ever written of a boiled dinner, but also a *pot-au-feu* that dared to include, with the authority of the greatest fictional gastronome who had ever lived, an entire foie gras poached in Chambertin! Devoted readers of this book treat these paragraphs as a recipe that any serious epicure is required to follow, at least once, in his or her continuing, if not lifelong, exploration of the *pot-au-feu*. My friends and I each prepared Dodin-Bouffant's *pot-au-feu*, and we all sort of succeeded.*

Then we moved on to the soubise, that fine onion purée Dodin serves to the Prince of Eurasia after the *pot-au-feu*, a lesson to both the Prince and to the rest of us that the low and humble onion, which would never have been considered fit for royalty, can grow epiphanous in the hands of a Dodin-Bouffant.† You will need an earthenware casserole, a quantity of new onions, the finest, freshest butter, thirty-six hours of free time, and a very low fire.

Who was Marcel Rouff? He was born in Geneva in 1887 and died in Paris in 1936. He was a poet, dramatist, essayist, literary critic, and chronicler of both the mountains and of Parisian society. If you browse library catalogues and the inventory of French dealers in rare books, you will discover: One volume of poetry. *Windmills,* an early one-act play in rhymed verse about Don Quixote, first pro-

---

* Lawrence Durrell's lovely Preface does not mention Dodin's *pot-au-feu*. "Claude," another Englishman, consistently chooses to translate the name of the dish as "boiled beef," even though a wide circle of delicate, poached sausage; an ample layer of chicken that has been raised only on bread and milk; and a slice of poached foie gras are crucial to the renown of Dodin's version.

Claude's translation of this passage is misleading, as it instructs us, in nearby sentences, that the beef itself is cut into the thinnest slices and that the slices are thick. (Claude's glossary at the back, not part of the original or any subsequent French edition, though purportedly prepared with advice from Elizabeth David, is also randomly accurate.) Durrell and Claude love this book for its literary value, not as a cookbook. But as most readers will surely strive to re-create Dodin's *pot-au-feu,* yet may lack even my mastery of Corneille and Racine, and easy access to the French text, I should mention that the slices of beef must be rather thick.

† Here the description is as clear as fine crystal.

duced at the Comédie de Genève, an apparent oxymoron; its first lines are spoken by Sancho Panza, and they concern food. A handful of novels, three now in print—Rouff's only writings still available. Biographies of Chateaubriand and of Tubeuf, a great industrialist of the eighteenth century, plus a study of French coal mines of the same era. And most notably, a series of delightful and gluttonous guides to the food of France, region by region, with recipes, written with the great and famous Curnonsky, the *nom de cuisine* of Maurice Edmond Sailland, honored throughout France as the Prince of Gourmets. (Several of the twenty-eight volumes of *La France Gastronomique, Guide des merveilles culinaires et des bonnes auberges françaises* were published in English by Harper and Brothers as *The Yellow Guides for Epicures*.) At the height of Curnonsky's prestige, eighty restaurants in and around Paris held back a table every night in case the Master should decide to show up.

Was the fictional Dodin-Bouffant modeled after a real-life gastronome? The action of the book appears to take place in the 1830s. (Here's how I figure it: Both Napoleon and the publication of the great Brillat-Savarin's *The Physiology of Taste* [1825], mentioned in the novel, have already happened, but the railroad has not yet arrived [probably 1842]; Dodin travels exclusively by carriage.) The setting is the Jura, a region of France given its title by the modest mountain range that runs along the Swiss border (and which also generously lends its name to the Jurassic Period and all that followed.) Just to the west lie the fertile gastronomic heartland of Burgundy, the city of Bresse, its fabled fowl, and the town of Belley, the seat of Brillat-Savarin himself and later of Lucien Tendret, another distinguished lawyer and author of the brilliant cookbook *La Table au Pays de Brillat-Savarin* (published in 1892 and reprinted in 1972), which later inspired a great mid-twentieth-century cook in the town of Mionnay, Alain Chapelle, and through him, the young

Alain Ducasse, who worked as Chapelle's *chef de cuisine* in the late 1970s. Alice B. Toklas, who with Gertrude Stein spent six months a year for seventeen years near Belley, boasts in her own cookbook of possessing and replicating one of Lucien Tendret's unpublished recipes. The French are proud of Alice and consider her a true disciple in the tradition of Belley and its surrounding countryside.

Brillat-Savarin and Tendret are the usual suspects. But Brillat-Savarin (to whom Rouff dedicates the book) is mentioned in the story as Dodin-Bouffant's *compatriote* and, in any event, was less of a homebody than Dodin. (Do you remember Brillat-Savarin's self-exile from the Terror, his sojourn in the United States, and his famous turkey shoot near Hartford, Connecticut?) Lucien Tendret came too late, and in any event, you will not find one dish in his cookbook that appears on Dodin's table. Alice B. Toklas has never been suggested. I would guess that it is both the unbroken tradition of Belley and its region, and Marcel Rouff's own gastronomic refinement and aphoristic skill that make up the person and manners of Dodin-Bouffant.

"I knew Marcel Rouff in the evening of his life," wrote James de Coquet in his Introduction to the 1970 French edition of *La Vie et la Passion de Dodin-Bouffant, Gourmet.* "He was a refined man, courteous, delicate, erudite, of whom one might say that he was the opposite of a gourmand.... When he knotted his napkin around his neck, in the manner of Brillat-Savarin, whose memory he venerated, it was to commune with nature, to incorporate her" (translation mine: caveat lector). This sounds like Dodin-Bouffant himself, except perhaps in the matter of physical size. But Coquet is probably too reverential. For one thing, we remember that Dodin-Bouffant "communes with nature" in the carriage on the way to the Prince's dinner by turning it into a meal: "The journey was enchanting.... There was joy at every turn of the road. Partridges ruffled the cornfields in their crazy race, like a breeze skimming the earth, and Dodin, pointing to a hare diving between a cow's muddy legs, beside the grey and tumbledown stones of a little vineyard wall, exclaimed: 'What admirable country! Look, Rabaz, at the marvellous combination: the creature, the cream, the wine: a complete jugged hare!' " For another, when we read Rouff's description of Dodin-Bouffant's apparent refinement at table, we understand that Rouff has concealed from Coquet his own obsessive gourmandism: "He [Dodin] was one of those men whose delicacy of manner and gesture, whose lightness of touch, whose distinction at table have so much charm that they conceal the extent of their appetite." Besides, everybody knows that truly delicate and ascetic men do not knot napkins around their necks.

Could you or I have won a place at Dodin's table? Frankly, I doubt it. Years ago, we read, Dodin "had welcomed to the succulence of his cuisine all those who craved the honour of tasting it." But as he grew older, his judgment became increasingly severe. "How many unworthy and inept false gourmets and vile flatterers had he seen trooping into his home!" So, he secretly began subjecting his guests to pitiless tests, and nearly all of them failed. One guest had taken an impeccable Châteauneuf-du-Pape for a Beaujolais, another failed to recognize "in the cream of a cauliflower sauce the exotic caress of a pinch of nutmeg," a third could not tell the difference between beef from Nivernais and beef from Franche-Comté, and a fourth "emptied a glass of Pommard after his coffee-cake"! Others were rejected for not having perceived a superfluous pinch of salt in a purée of cardoons, or for having mistakenly praised the badly buttered toast "under a partridge of the wrong age."

Only four men survived, and they now dine together once a

week at Dodin-Bouffant's house: Beaubois the notary, Magot the cattle dealer, Trifouille the municipal librarian, and Rabaz, a doctor in whom Dodin has too little faith to entrust his own painful case of gout but to whom he would surely entrust his dinner. Whether the five are capable of conducting a conversation on any subject other than food is doubtful. What they do before or after eating, if there is a before or an after, is not known. Dodin himself appears to have a rich fantasy life in sexual matters, but their consummation has been strictly utilitarian and limited to two cooks in his employ. And at the end of the novel, he turns down a coupling that might have rivaled the union of Dido and Aeneas. This is not to say that a really, really fine meal cannot beat out Dido and Aeneas any day of the year. But it shows why the question of whether Dodin-Bouffant belongs in the ranks of Falstaff and Mr. Pickwick or only of D'Artagnan, or whether he is truly the Dr. Johnson of the dinner table, is off the point. Dodin is less a literary character and more an idea and an ideal, a limiting case, a life gone to extremes, a reductio ad absurdum.

Those of us who are only slightly less obsessed and monomaniacal than he—including Marcel Rouff—need frequent assurance that our own singlemindedness is neither frivolous nor sinful. Despite what Thoreau tells us ("He who distinguishes the true savor of his food can never be a glutton; he who does not cannot be otherwise"), the deadly sin of gluttony consists not only in the amount we eat but also in the attention we lavish on fine distinctions. C. S. Lewis calls this the sin (or sub-sin) of "delicacy." Even a possible aesthete such as Marcel Rouff knows he is in mortal danger, unless he can find a way out.

And the way out is to define gastronomy as an art. When a painter ignores his quotidian existence to lie on his back for two years and paint the pope's ceiling, we gasp in admiration for his purity and dedication and zeal. In theory at least, art excuses nearly anything. The status of cooking and gastronomy is an issue that all of us who give over our lives to eating have long pondered; in my experience, the skeptics too frequently have the best of the argument. But Rouff argues the case, both in his "Apologia" (in this edition, moved from the beginning of the book to the end) and in the story itself (in his oration at the funeral of his longtime cook, Eugénie Chatagne, for example), more persuasively and more beautifully than any other author I know. Three conditions must be met: the sense of taste must be put on a par with our other senses; it must be capable of the same subtle manipulation as all the others; and the entire enterprise of gastronomy must be seen to possess a meaning, an emotional and moral content. At least that's how I've always figured it.

On the first point, Dodin wins the day. He talks of the "inconceivable aberration which denies to the sense of taste the faculty of engendering an art, whereas no one denies this faculty to the senses of sight and hearing.... Our sensibility is a single entity. Who cultivates it, cultivates the whole of it, and I insist that he is a false artist who is not also a gourmet, and a false gourmet who can see no beauty in a colour and find no emotion in a sound.... Art is the understanding of beauty through the senses, through all the senses...."

Addressing the second test, Dodin praises the departed Eugénie for virtues traditionally associated with artists. She is a "treasury of inventiveness," and possesses a "precious gift for matching tones, flavours and their nuances, an incomparable intuition for measure, harmony, the balance of likes and opposites, in short the genius of appealing, in order to satisfy them, to all the exigencies of our sensibility: are these then the exclusive perquisites of the blenders of colours or the makers of sounds?"

Whether the discoveries and pleasures of gastronomy are capable of deeper meaning—that is the remaining question. Rouff completes his tale with a moral lesson. Dodin is understandably drawn to a brilliant and lovely young admirer, Pauline, and their meeting, their moments of bi-sensual frenzy, are so well depicted as to arouse every reader. Then Dodin draws back, thinking of the pain he would cause to his wife, to Pauline, and even to himself. "She [Pauline] had thought to attack and carry off Dodin Bouffant with the complicity of his exalted senses; she had not divined that sensuality, when it rises above itself, has a morality and a purity of its own. She had seen Dodin-Bouffant, the epicure, on earth, but had failed to see Dodin-Bouffant, the apostle, among the stars."

Does this mean that the morality of the obsessive gourmet consists in pushing himself away from the table? Not a very persuasive argument. We appreciate what Marcel Rouff is trying to do. We feel his guilt. But it all seems unnecessary (and a bit high-flown) to justify some of the finest and most enticing writing about food you'll ever find. Heaven can wait.

—

JEFFREY STEINGARTEN is *Vogue* magazine's food critic and author of *The Man Who Ate Everything* and *It Must've Been Something I Ate*. He trained to be a food writer on the *Harvard Lampoon*. On Bastille Day, 1994, the French Republic made Mr. Steingarten a Chevalier in the Order of Merit for his writings on French gastronomy. Chevalier Steingarten discloses that his preferred eating destinations are Memphis, Paris, Bangkok, Alba, Chengdu—and his loft in New York City. His articles in *Vogue* have recently won a National Magazine Award.

Contents

PREFACE

Lawrence Durrell

When a writer manages to put an arrow successfully through the centre of a national strength or weakness, the result is often a masterpiece, and while I cannot claim for Marcel Rouff's creation the symbolic universality of characters like Falstaff, Pickwick, Oblomov or Quixote, I believe I could make out a very fair case for regarding him (despite the slenderness of this book) as being as much a true finding as D'Artagnan, Tartarin and our own beloved Mr Sponge. The deities of the second magnitude are no less companionable than their seniors for all who love literature.

The portentous, magistral figure of Dodin-Bouffant looms gravely over the Olympus of gastronomy like a sort of Zeus. He is the French Doctor Johnson of the table, exciting both laughter and tenderness. His amatory no less than his gastronomic predicaments are as well chosen to illustrate his epicurean philosophy as Rouff's misty-eyed oratorical prose is to describe (you almost feel) the very outlines of the Master's vast circumambient rotundities.

Hovering as the book does between gravity and mockery, it nevertheless hides under its smiling exterior a highly civilized philosophy of the French table and the French heart. Why should it not? Marcel Rouff, its author, is already known to us. Together with his old *confrère* and friend Curnonsky ('*Le Prince des Gastronomes*') he is responsible for the compilation of that unique work *La France Gastronomique,* a work not likely to be superseded in its field in our generation. What happy years those two *fervents* must have passed in examining, in the minutest and most mouth-watering detail, the whole tremendously varied and idiosyncratic apparatus of French cookery. They left (to judge by the fruits of all this convivial research) no crumb unturned, and their master-work is as near perfect as human endeavour could make it. Somewhere, purely on the side, perhaps even as a joke, Dodin-Bouffant got himself born. I privately suspect that his portrait owes something to Brillat-Savarin to whom the first edition was dedicated, for the author of *La Physiologie du Goût* resembled Dodin-Bouffant both in resilient avoirdupois and oratorical splendour: not to mention in wholehearted devotion to the science of the table. A fitting patron saint for a gastronome! The Brillat-Savarins came of heroic stock and all died at the dinner-table, fork in hand. Brillat's great-aunt, for example, died at the age of 93 while sipping a glass of old Virieu, while Pierrette, his sister, two months before her hundredth birthday, uttered (at table) the following last words which are forever enshrined in the memory of good Frenchmen: '*Vite,*' she cried, '*apportez-moi le dessert—je sens que je vais passer!*' Dodin-Bouffant is a fitting tribute to such giants.

The destiny of a good book is often a strange one. One would, for example, have imagined Dodin-Bouffant to become immediately a *livre de chevet* for all clear-minded Frenchmen. Not a bit of it. The first edition went out of print and stayed out of print. He is impossible to find in Paris today, except perhaps in a private library. Now, however, by a curious twist of fate, he is to be resurrected in London. I think this important fact should be regarded as an Augury, a Sign, for it is certainly a fact that since the end of the war cookery in England has taken several big strides forward; a new spirit of confidence and adventure is abroad, thanks no doubt to the work of such great religious pioneers as Mr Simon and Miss Elizabeth David among others. At any rate, it would be possible to invite Dodin today to a meal in London which (would he admit it?) was touched with the right sort of sensuality. Much remains to be done. But now we have a Master to guide our steps. It is pleasing, too, to steal a short march on our keen-eyed, curious and generous French neighbours across the Channel who have so mysteriously overlooked and neglected this little masterpiece. In an age for which Trimalchio is perhaps the most fitting symbol we need our perspectives corrected by this great virtuoso of the table. I think that Rouff sums him up perfectly when he says: '*C'est un sage et c'est un vieux Français.*'

THE PASSIONATE EPICURE

1

Four Artists and Eugenie Chatagne

A burning summer noon sets the Town Hall square, quite deserted, afire with light; the only signs of life are given by baked and dusty limes. Heat and emptiness have invaded the tiny Café de Saxe, an inn where the Duc de Courlande, on long-ago provincial visits, would sometimes condescend to restore himself with a fricassee and three flasks of some fresh local wine.

In there, the darkness induced by grimy yellowish blinds, is punctuated by the dark stains of four plush-covered benches, of the worn marble of table-tops, and the red, green and yellow transparencies of the syrups, apéritifs and liqueurs throwing a multicoloured alcoholic halo around the landlord. He sits behind his counter in shirt-sleeves, fat and shiny, bald and morose, upon a high stool protectively fenced-in by a pyramid of glasses.

Despite his spasmodic efforts to dismiss the cloud of flies intent upon the folds in his flesh, he displays an unwonted reserve, heavy with a vague distress, an unspoken anguish.

This anguish, this distress, are also clearly uppermost in the souls of two customers pondering a common concern over empty coffee-cups, surrounded by a complicated apparatus of boxes, spirit-stoves and containers which have just aided the preparation of the precious liquid.

The thinner—or perhaps the less stout—of the two, his long arms stretched across the marble table, raises a head of extreme whiteness as to hair and redness as to complexion, revealing a face whose salient feature is the mouth: lips so peculiar as to arrest one's attention, long thin lips which seem eternally to be savouring a nectar completely perfect.

'And what about Dodin? How will he face up to the blow? It means the disruption of his whole existence!'

These sombre words, spoken by Magot in a tremulous voice, fall into a silence which not even the indomitable fly-buzzing can disturb.

Magot slumps on the bench, allowing the protrusion of a paunch which, without as yet appearing grotesque, seems to offer to invisible fanciers a blatant if imaginary gold chain, spanning its gentle curves. He chews a dangling moustache, one of those moustaches which inevitably drip wine after drinking, inevitably present their owners with the alternatives of avoiding the most succulent soups or bankrupting themselves at the dry-cleaners'. His small, sensuous eyes have an odd look when, as now, sorrow dims their customary twinkle. He is obviously the prey of one of those fat men's sorrows which can be a shade ridiculous.

'Ah! I daren't think of it,' answers Beaubois, after a pause.

Beaubois is a notary, Magot a cattle-dealer.

14

The threat of unhappiness suspended over the inn has affected the only two other customers; slightly apart, in the expectation of an event which they await albeit in ignorance of its nature, they have paused in their game of cards; these passing visitors, commercial travellers whose vulgarity fades into inconspicuousness in the atmosphere of catastrophe weighing upon the town, are somewhat embarrassed to witness as strangers the forebodings of a great and intimate sorrow.

Yes, weighing upon the town, for the passers-by, few at this stifling hour, move slowly, greeting each other with mere nods, and crossing the square side-by-side to halt at the threshold of the café, not entering, but making interrogative, news-hungry head-signs to the landlord (himself rather proud, after all, of his involvement in the affair). Then they throw Beaubois and Magot one of those indefinable looks by which men convey sympathy for the imminent suffering of others and congratulate themselves upon being spared.

Unconsciously, from habit and to ease the waiting, to console himself, Beaubois yet again refills a wineglass with the thick golden liquid poured from a bellying bottle; idly he reads its label which he knows by heart, sniffs the rim of the glass which his closed fist shelters, tilts it, touches the drink with his tongue, and closes his eyes.

'Fifty-six! That's not old?'

The strollers, still very few although two o'clock has struck, pause suddenly to converse quietly together and then fall into step behind Doctor Rabaz as he crosses the square in a hurry, bent double, head lowered in the pompous and thoughtful manner proper to bearers of grave tidings or to people in the grip of pressing abdominal problems.

Some question him; he only nods in reply. He appears choked

15

with emotion, and holds in one hand a large handkerchief with which he mops up tears or sweat—who knows which? The other hand is pressed to an indeterminate part of his body which may be his heart or his stomach.

The landlord of the Café de Saxe, watching his arrival from afar, says casually to Magot and Beaubois (to prepare them for the inevitable): 'The doctor!'

And these two are already on their feet, heading for the door, arms dangling, eyes doubtful and bewildered.

The landlord has left his counter; the commercial travellers, without quite knowing why, have risen, and it is to these five men, their nerves taut from long waiting, that Doctor Rabaz, pausing at the steps, hat in hand, tensely and automatically wiping his glistening face, announces:

'It is all over. She has just passed away. . . .'

Adding, pointlessly, for listeners no longer listening, the vague medical explanation: 'It was a burst varicose vein.'

The café relapses into a sombre stupor, sunk after this brief scene into the silence of grieving, so different from that of suspense. For now sorrow really is there, a presence. But at least it is something known, no longer apprehended. The threat has materialized, has declared itself, and fear no longer hovers. A measure of relief dawns, a shifting of emotion within some kind of certainty.

The commercial travellers, excluded from the mourning group, have regained the distant encampment of their glasses, cups, newspapers, directories and cards, when the landlord, buttoning his waistcoat to confer a suitable dignity upon the occasion, and thus to underline the fact that he is no stranger to the tragedy, approaches. They ask: 'Was it really . . .?'

'Don't ask me, my dear sirs; it is an irreparable loss. These

16

gentlemen' (indicating Beaubois, Magot and the doctor), 'are probably the greatest gourmets in France; there is no connoisseur to equal them in the kingdom. Good heavens, if only you could have heard them after each meal concocted by that artist! Pro- digious . . . it was simply prodigious! I myself have had the honour of sampling her cooking. Monsieur Dodin-Bouffant, on one occasion when I had managed to procure him a prune *ratafia* distilled in 1798, sent me a pâté of turkey breasts in Madeira. Ah, gentlemen! The man who has not tasted. . . .'

Rabaz, Beaubois and Magot discussed the death-agony in low voices. The doctor's technical details blended strangely with memories of impeccable wild ducks, of unbeatable white truffles, of roe tarts and of rabbits 'Père Douillet', of fowls 'at day- break' . . . and the three men, even Rabaz whose puffy bearded face reflected the sceptical and blasé materialism of old doctors who have witnessed many deaths, felt the warm gush of tears behind their eyelids.

And indeed, why should they not? Eugénie Chatagne, cook to Dodin-Bouffant, was dead. In the full flower of her genius she had vanished; incomparable artist, blessed dispenser of all those culinary delights of which, at the table of a master famous in the whole of France, they had been the profoundly gratified beneficiaries! Exceptionally endowed with those qualities which make for great gastronomic achievement she had, under the direction of the king of gourmets, the lord of perfect eating, lavished upon them the rarest of sensations, the most thrilling experiences; she had exalted them, blissful souls, to the highest peaks of cloudless joy. Eugénie Chatagne, inspired interpreter of the superior intentions which Nature has implanted in all foodstuffs, had, by employment of refinements, display of talent, application of, resort to infallible taste and perfection of execution, wrenched cooking away from the materialistic sphere to raise it, sovereign and absolute, to the most transcendent regions which humanity can envisage.

Was it not to her that the three of them owed their initiation into the great cult, their development into competent, nay superlative, judges, into *amateurs* who had achieved scientific infallibility? Had she not opened their eyes to the true direction their lives should take? Had she not formed their palates as a musician forms the ear of a pupil, a painter the eye of a disciple? Now they remember, and the tears which foolish self-consciousness holds back behind their smarting eyelids bespeak grateful recognition of the feasts of yore, and gratitude for the future delights for which she had prepared them. Under Dodin-Bouffant's erudite tuition, she had prodigiously enlarged her native genius, acquired a mastery, a self-confidence, a scientific skill in handling and combining flavours which had made her famous from Chambéry to Besançon, from Dijon to Geneva, in that region of Europe where cookery has incontrovertibly reached its zenith. Eugénie Chatagne was as famous in the region as her master, Dodin-Bouffant himself, the Napoleon of gourmets, the Beethoven of cooking, the Shakespeare of the table! Princes had tried in vain to force the door of that simple dining-room to which only three guests, tried, true, and entirely worthy, were admitted. But what complete and utter joys these elect few had tasted there! Today, they weep over these memories, and over recollections of all the friendly intimacy and contentment which for any man of heart and spirit accompany the powerful aroma of an old Burgundy, or the divine earthy fragrance of a perfect truffle. To procure them these joys, had not Eugénie, dear Eugénie, refused the offers of a sovereign, a cardinal and a minister?

Suddenly Rabaz, attempting to master his grief, says sadly: 'Dodin's expecting you—he asked me to bring you over.'

Resignedly, Beaubois and Magot take their hats from the rack, tremulous at the prospect of confronting their friend's sorrow.

In the climbing street, several people stood about, already commenting on the event. They threw furtive, sympathetic glances at the house where Dodin-Bouffant mourned, and greeted the three friends respectfully as they went on their way, puffing a little. Before the closed shutters under the modest porch of the house of mourning, Beaubois stopped anxiously, hat in hand, to express the thought common to these epicures, unaccustomed to the notion of death:

'There are no pronouncements to be made—there is nothing to be said.'

They found the front door ajar and went into the passage at the end of which a glass door revealed a small but well-stocked garden; the familiar belongings of the owner, his hat, his stick, his coat, wore an abandoned, an infinitely sad aspect, an air of weariness and catastrophe.

There were two doors on the right; on the left a door and a staircase opened on to this narrow corridor, furnished only with a coat-rack. Magot, secretly hoping that Dodin would not be behind it, softly opened the right-hand door, which squeaked pitilessly. He was afraid now, hideously afraid to face this man whose life had suddenly been shattered.

Dodin was striding back and forth in his library, hands behind his back, solemn in a black frock coat. Around his neck rose a double cravat of satin, also black; his handsome face, clean-shaven and framed in white mutton-chop whiskers, gave evidence of immense self-control. (Beaubois sighed with relief at having made this first contact.) All the delicacy of this countenance, its refinement and its intelligent sensuality, were shadowed by a bravely-contained but overwhelming distress; the upper lip, full, greedy and aristocratic, quivered in a repressed sob. In the half-shade of the room, famous menus framed and hung upon the walls between racy engravings showed up as darker patches. Stray beams of light played upon the old gold-ornamented bindings of the books.

In silence the master extended a hand to the companions who had shared his grand and noble repasts, and resumed his monotonous pacing. As he crossed and re-crossed the room, his gaze wandered over the shelves where old books, the great classics of wit and *cuisine*, were lovingly arrayed. At last he sat down at the desk, leaning his elbows on the scattered papers, chin in hand, and his eyes went to a special shelf. The glances of his friends followed the same direction: there they all were, in their pink and green paper covers, or their dark calf bindings, those famous books: *Court Suppers*, *Bourgeois Cuisine*, *The Physiology of Taste*, the *Gourmet's Almanack*, the *Imperial Cook*, the *Encyclopaedia of Famous Cookery*, and so many more, the glorious traditions of the old French provinces in their safe keeping for future generations. Almost daily, during the long years of their collaboration, Eugénie had studied the pages of these magnificent annals of an unrecognized art, an art achieving the unlikely synthesis of liveliness, refinement, good manners and the delicious light-heartedness of the gallo-latin race.

Dodin-Bouffant, in that hour of mourning, contemplated this precious corner of his library where he had so lovingly accumulated the materials for the ephemeral, yet perpetually renewed, the glorious and unfailing masterpieces which, with the now dead woman at his side, he had created.

A retired county magistrate, sprung from old and influential legal stock, he had inherited, together with a serene philosophy of life and a certain sceptical indulgence in judging others, an atavistic taste for generous and epicurean living. The loss of an assistant with talents commensurate with his own genius wounded him in his deepest and most stubborn instincts. Yes, I say genius, for could one refuse that supreme and solemn homage to the qualities which he had dedicated to the culinary art, after thirty years of practising human justice? Yes, genius, that astonishing combination in performance as in principle, of custom and innovation, tradition and bold departures therefrom, of ritual and fantasy! Genius, the prodigious faculty of creation framed in considered and immutable principles, with its sense of harmony, its profound penetration of character, and of character's requirements, of circumstances and their consequences; genius, the protean discoveries of his imagination!

It was to these natural dispositions that society was indebted both for judgements inspired by profound juridical knowledge and great human mercy (which had left their mark upon the Law) and for gastronomic inventions of unfailing boldness and brilliance: Dodin-Bouffant, before all others, had dared to wed fish and fowl, for example, and enhance the aroma of a capon, copiously marinated, by a stuffing in which the dominant notes were the flavours of shrimps and turbot.

His eyes moved from the bookshelves to Rabaz, Magot and Beaubois, still as mummies upon the sofa which was shaped like a large conch-shell, only their hats revolving between their anguished fingers.

'Come and see her,' he said suddenly.

Deeply moved, they crossed the hallway to enter the drawing-room. All the old-fashioned furniture, of yellow and blue striped repp in massive walnut frames, had been pushed into the shadowy corners. At the end of the room, fitful and funereal, the lonely light of candles fell uncertain and yellowish upon the dead woman's face: poor thing, grown suddenly youthful, almost smiling in the dawn of an oblivion that lightened the tired mask of fifty years. From this face framed in a fluted white bonnet and chestnut hair, shone an unmistakable nobility, a refinement full of good humour. To look upon it was to sense a solid understanding of material generosity, an assured instinct for comfort. It was a face to reassure you on the threshold of an inn.

On a table near the corpse, beside the holy water, Dodin had arranged what remained upon this earth of the poor body's masterpieces: her triumphant menus, copper-plated upon stiff pasteboard. A neighbour prayed. A huge fly buzzed about the room unendurably, banging into walls, window-panes, lamp-shades. No one dared disturb its improper saraband.

'Rabaz,' said Dodin-Bouffant, turning slowly towards the doctor after lengthy contemplation of the deceased, 'inform the undertaker that I wish to speak at the cemetery.'

Dodin-Bouffant did indeed speak at the graveside. The whole population of the small town had joined him for the funeral. He considered it was honouring the dead publicly to outline the greatness of the art which she had adorned, to set out its main principles, to extract its philosophy, and restore to cookery in the vulgar mind the dignity to which it had every right. And there, in the humble provincial cemetery, tranquil, beflowered, shaded and cooled by a neighbouring stream, he gave of his heart far better than he had ever done during the solemn sessions when, under the aegis of the Law, he was wont to begin from the ascendency of the Presidential seat: 'Ladies and Gentlemen . . .'

'Ladies and Gentlemen, . . .' he now began,

'For me, the funeral of Eugénie Chatagne must be an apotheosis. It is my fervent and sorrowful wish. I shall mourn my devoted collaborator of so many years' standing, rendering to the generous efforts of her whole life the homage which some would unjustly deny her. I speak, Ladies and Gentlemen, for the culinary art, demanding that it be granted its proper place beside its peers, the other major arts, among the great achievements of human culture. I affirm that, were it not for an inconceivable aberration which denies to the sense of taste the faculty of engendering an art, whereas no one denies this faculty to the senses of sight and hearing, Eugénie Chatagne would have an assured place in the same company as our great painters and musicians.

'A treasury of inventiveness, a precious gift for matching tones, flavours and their nuances, an incomparable intuition for measure, harmony, the balance of likes and opposites, in short the genius of appealing, in order to satisfy them, to all the exigences of our sensibility: are these then the exclusive perquisites of the blenders of colours or the makers of sounds? Ephemeral works, you will say, those of the table! Works with no tomorrows, soon buried by forgetful time! Works more durable, surely, than those of the virtuosi and actors you acclaim. The genial discoveries of a Carême or a Vatel, the prodigious findings of a Grimod de la Reynière or a Brillat-Savarin, are they not still alive among you? Many paintings by masters of a day have disappeared from the sight of men, and yet we still enjoy the satin-smooth *purée* of Soubise's chef, or chicken as it was cooked for the victor of Marengo. Gentlemen, I leave to those who profess that man eats only to sustain himself the shame of declining into cave-man primitiveness. Those and their kind must also prefer to Lully or Beethoven a blast on an auroch's horn, and to Watteau or Poussin the rough cave drawings of prehistoric beings. Our sensibility is a single entity. Who cultivates it, cultivates the whole of it, and I insist that he is a false artist who is not also a gourmet, and a false gourmet who can see no beauty in a colour and find no emotion in a sound.

'Art is the understanding of beauty through the senses, through all the senses, and in order to understand the dream of a Vinci, or the inner life of a Bach, one must, I repeat, be capable of adoring the scented and fugitive soul of a passionate wine.

'It is a great artist, Ladies and Gentlemen, that we mourn today. For many years Eugénie Chatagne studied an art which also has its patents of nobility. Her memory will live among men. My pious hands and grateful heart will erect to her, with the materials she has left behind and which I have assembled, the monument she deserves, the book she will sign from the depths of the grave, the book more permanent than stone or metal which will hand on to posterity the essence of her genius.

'Ladies and Gentlemen, should France ever forsake the great culinary traditions which Eugénie Chatagne so nobly represented, she would destroy a vital element of her prestige, deny one of the finest jewels in her crown. I am at an age when one loves old books, and without quoting from accounts our ancestors have given of themselves, I call upon the travellers, the foreign travellers, of the past centuries. Their memoirs, their letters, show that on the threshold of their own countries, their peregrinations at an end, they would turn back one last time towards the Kingdom of France and fill their hearts once more with the sense of its power, their eyes with the light of its sky, and their nostrils with the delicate scent of all the savoury victuals issued from its soil.

'One of these visitors, in the sixteenth century, mentions the rôtisseries and the cellars of France in the same breath as her marvellous castles and the sweetness of her countryside. In the seventeenth century, another waxes lyrical over Louis XIV's military power, the excellence of the inns, and the genius of our great authors. In the eighteenth century, numberless tourists who visit the kingdom extol all the gastronomic products of the provinces; others swear they have drunk the soul of France at the Clos du Roi of Vosne Romanée, and eaten her flesh at the glorious tables of every inn they have visited.

'Ladies and Gentlemen, in my affliction it would be unseemly for me to develop further the extent of my thoughts before this grave so soon to be closed. I wished to offer the dead my homage and my admiration. Flashes of our national genius sprang from you, Eugénie Chatagne. Steady and high you bore the standard of an art which, like all arts, has its great men and its martyrs, its inspirations and its doubts, its joys and sorrows. The earth is about to receive a noble woman whose place is among the foremost creators of culture and human refinement.'

That evening all the cooks of the town, which boasts many a famous one, approached their stoves with dreamy gravity, and some of them saw the dawn of rehabilitation in the ardent coals.

2

Dodin's Dilemma

F or some time after the death of Eugénie Chatagne Dodin-Bouffant took his meals at the Café de Saxe, bringing anguish and terror into that peaceful establishment. Twice a day, to the dining-room where the famous gourmet sat severe and inscrutable, the trembling cook dispatched feverishly-concocted dishes; the innkeeper, in an attempt to conceal his unease and his constant fear of an explosion of contempt, plunged into his book-keeping: the figures danced before his eyes as he waited at every moment for the irritable voice of his client to be raised. Dodin-Bouffant, resignedly, said not a word.

Convinced, however, that he owed it to the memory of the departed to uphold and preserve from decay an art which she had adorned, and determined, moreover, to eat as decently as heretofore, after a week of mortification he caused an advertisement to be inserted in the front page of the regional newspaper, in which he declared in solemn terms that a high standard had been set for those of good will who wished to follow in great

footsteps, and that he would welcome such as already had serious experience and a sincere passion for the cult to which they made sacrifice.

In all sincerity, he dared not hope that a second Eugénie Chatagne would come to embellish his existence, nor simultaneously to satisfy his aesthetic taste for superior cookery and, it must be admitted, the coarser requirements of his other senses which had retained much of their youthfulness but to which a provincial career had offered satisfactions of mediocre quality. Eugénie Chatagne had, beyond possible doubt, added to her culinary virtuosity an amiable personal capitulation not devoid of charm at the still tender age when she entered the service of the former magistrate.

As a smiling philosopher, convinced that one must never ask life twice in succession to provide exceptional blessings and the good fortune of finding upon one's way an elect being capable at the same time of dispensing the joys of the heart and the pleasures of the flesh, Dodin was firmly resolved, should he succeed in finding the germ of a fine culinary talent, to nourish from separate sources the appetites which his late cook had satisfied in her own sole person.

The bold applicants who presented themselves for the master's interviews had mostly a very high opinion of themselves. Some of them, embarking upon the venture, thought secretly that the refinement of the house had been exaggerated by hearsay. Others, crossing the threshold, had not the simplest or slightest notion of their own temerity.

Dodin would receive the candidate in his library. As she entered, he would rise politely and, in doubt giving her the benefit of possible genius, beg her to be seated in a comfortable armchair; whilst he inquired most tactfully about her age, her family, her living conditions, her former employment, his juridical eye would rest upon each feature through which a culinary artist might reveal herself. Above all, he would survey the mouth at great length, and if the lips were fleshy, note their shape in search of that mobility which is a sign of sharpened senses, that quiver which suggests the habitual development of an organ, in short, he sought that physiognomy of greed which constitutes an initial guarantee. He immediately eliminated square and pointed chins, requiring of them a roundness which would reassure him as to the necessary degree of sensuality. In their eyes too he read things which are indefinable, but which did not lead him astray.

If this first examination suggested to him no peremptory reasons for prolonging it, he found a canny pretext for breaking it off. When, on the other hand, he decided that further investigation was worth while, he would lead the conversation in a grave tone towards gastronomical considerations, and, although he did not expect from his visitors either profound thoughts or new, skilfully expressed views, upon the technique of their art, he knew very well how to discern, even from brief, awkward or clumsy responses, what he could hope of the good woman's intelligence, instinct and vocation. Sometimes he would emit some heresy in order to elicit a revealing protest, at others he would firmly state his preference for charcoal-cooked meat, or proclaim the necessity for suiting the essence of the firewood to the nature of the meat to be cooked. And even if he observed his candidates' ignorance of these elementary truths, at least he noted the effect of his statements upon them, and from their attitudes deduced their faculties of assimilation and what promise they might hold out. Sometimes, in the middle of the conversation, he would rise, walk over to the favourite shelves of his library, select therefrom a rare volume of the *Almanach des Gourmands*, open it with the deft gesture of a habitual book-handler, and say: 'Grimod de la Reynière wrote: "Sixth year. Chapter on Bindings. The immoderate use of *roux* and *coulis* has formed all the charlatanism of French cuisine for the past hundred years."' Holding the book open, head bent, but looking over his spectacles at the bewildered girl, he would add: 'Grimod, with good reason, chose this essential observation from *La Cuisine de Santé*, Tome 1, p. 247. Meditate, Mademoiselle, meditate!' And he would add, continuing to read, '*Some* flour and certain starches employed with moderation, real meat and game gravies, essences and well-reduced stocks often enter into the composition of bindings. It is from the art of skilful blending that a good binding draws its principal value, and this is a difficult art. However, if a binding is not perfect, it separates instead of uniting, and as it is the complement of the *ragoût*, if it adds not to its perfection it must surely ruin it.' He would close the book and narrowly watch the effect of this high technique upon his possible cook.

To tell the truth, most of them, upon hearing these philosophical meditations, seemed to be seized by sudden cramp in the buttocks, performing a giratory but stationary movement upon their chairs. In fact, they would have been far happier elsewhere. The unconscious and ignorant began to be enlightened. The confident made the acquaintance of doubt; some remained dumbfounded; a few, finally, were made aware of great gulfs of science which filled them with a passing vertigo. These last Dodin identified easily. He retained them only, and mercifully, to rescue them from the grip of their discomfort and bring them down to earth again, putting the book back in its place he would suggest a visit to the 'laboratory', that is to say, the kitchen. He took them first to the dining-room, furnished in light oak, bright, cheerful and comfortable, inciting by its gentle atmosphere a flow of beautiful inspirations. The table could hold no more than a limited number of guests, eight at most. He pointed at it:

'It must always be adorned by flowers as well as by china, so that the senses may be amused and rested, but not distracted: they must remain concentrated upon the main object.'

The sideboard and side-table, bearing massive pieces of family plate, were broad, convenient, and well set out to accommodate a number of dishes with ease. The glassware, in neat rows of thick ribbed crystal, and very wide-mouthed, was designed to welcome the appreciative nose as well as the grateful lip. The armchairs were built to favour supreme ease of the posterior. A few field flowers, upon a small occasional table of no particular period, bowed over the lip of a stoneware jar.

A very large bay occupied the entire rear of the room, opening upon a very small but very green garden, carefully tended and brightened by flowering gladioli and budding geraniums. A delicious temperature reigned in this room the whole year round: the sixteen degrees centigrade which a wood-fire maintained in winter were retained in summer by a somewhat elaborate system of draughts. Upon the walls were two etchings of a rather risky nature, a dry-point portrait of Grimod, and a painting in which a covey of quail was represented in the shadow of a luminous copper cauldron.

The aspiring cook was invariably greatly moved on entering the kitchen. Suddenly, whatever her normal opinion of herself, she felt minute, humble, non-existent.

It was of vast proportions, this kitchen, well-lit by large windows with fine screens allowing ingress to the air whilst forbidding it to flies. The eye was drawn at once to an immense range: it occupied the entire wall and ended with a well-filled wood-box. Beside it, a door opened outwards on to the garden fountain. This stove comprised a gigantic spit, seconded by a smaller one, two ovens (one of which was a field-oven, designed to allow a dish to cook above and below simultaneously). Three openings for hot, medium and cool fires. There was also all the equipment for cooking fish, and a special section for pastry. Finally, an entire section of the huge stove was fitted for open-fire cooking. Beside it, within comfortable reach of the execu-tant, a veritable library housed an infinite variety of ingredients, spices, peppers, aromatics, jars of glazes, vinegars and wines, syrups—all carefully labelled. A large, bright dish-holder over-flowed with china; another table for chopping and cutting, and another, lighter but of a fair size, seemed lost in the enormous temple. Two superimposed shelves displayed a crowd of cast-iron pots, saucepans, earthenware containers, pie-dishes, frying-pans, skillets, stew-pots and soup-kettles. Copper, formerly somewhat rare, had gradually multiplied in this kitchen: Dodin had realized at last that earthenware, which he had long pre-ferred, tended in the long run to absorb the flavour of greasy molecules retained in its pores. Outside the windows there were flowers. Two notices stood out sharply upon the fresh walls. One read as follows: 'The most meticulous cleanliness is compulsory.' And the other: 'The use of bottled essences for seasonings and sauces is forbidden and will lead to instant dismissal.'

In this sanctuary the visitor, at first intimidated and then frankly terrified, at last suspected the complexity and refinement of a prodigious art, and upon discovering the grandeur and the gravity of her mission, soon lost her head. The encouraging words of Dodin-Bouffant, hardly piercing her uneasy dizziness, could not restore her serenity.

'You are moved by the ghost of the greatness that reigned here. But if you settle down in the "workshop" it will become a familiar and helpful counsellor to you. Your personality will acquire strength, and affirm itself. Here, you might even create some masterpieces!'

When the master and his possible collaborator had returned to the library, Dodin would allow peace to flow back into the soul of the unhappy candidate who would instantly have declined the fearsome honour of catering for the gastronomic joys of so prodigious an epicure, were it not for the immense moral benefit she believed could ensue, for the whole of her life, from serving such a master. Perhaps too, in the least noble and most materialistic part of her heart, she may have considered the profits to be derived from these daily banquets. Moreover, other things apart, the wages were most attractive.

After a moment of silent thought, Dodin-Bouffant would resume:

'Allow me, my child' (he spoke thus even to the most elderly), 'allow me to ask you a few questions. I apologize for doing so, but it is supremely important that we should be well-informed about each other.'

He spoke with respect to these women, fearing to show irreverence, without wishing it, to some unknown great artist who might not even suspect her own capacities, and he treated them as equals.

'A good meal, my child, must harmonize with the age, the social condition and the state of mind of the persons invited to enjoy it.'

He did not hope to encounter the exceptional being so intuitive as to have discovered alone this refined rule of gastronomy, and relied, in this so delicate region of the ordering of meals, only upon his own experience, his personal taste, and his education. But he may still perhaps have hoped for the impossible miracle, and have wished to ascertain the extent to which instinct did service for science in his candidates.

The wide-eyed would-be cook often felt a 'little death', a cold shiver trickle moistly down her spine.

'Supposing,' pursued Dodin, 'that I wish to entertain a few middle-aged bachelors, doctors and business-men, who rejoice in domestic pleasures. . . . Do not be alarmed, my girl, . . . answer. . . .'

Dodin-Bouffant, approving, correcting or helping the patient, would compose an ideal menu, as an examiner himself formulates the reply of an interesting candidate. He analysed the reasons for his choice, assorted the order of the dishes to the character and private life of each of the supposed guests. When, in the course of these laborious obstetrical operations, he uncovered a few elements which allowed him to hope for future results of an appreciable nature from methodical education and his own competent direction, he would add:

'We have barely touched upon theory, my child. We may perhaps get on together, especially if you consent to work docilely under my inspiration. But I must submit you to a practical test. Come tomorrow at eight. You will prepare my luncheon which is served precisely at twelve. At seven, upon rising, I eat only eggs and sausages. My charwoman can manage that quite well at the moment.'

Dodin-Bouffant drained the cup to the dregs. For days he tasted the test-meals with horror and patience; sautéed chickens tactlessly stifled under mountains of tomatoes, shamefully bungled stews, dry, curled-up partridges, veal fricassees in watery unbound gravy devoid of all creaminess, hare robbed of its gamy aroma, soggy fried potatoes, un-buttered butter-beans! As if, in the land of France, where great cooking is after all a national art, the hoped-for cook must remain unfindable for the great man.

One must add, however, that the impeccable, the genial Dodin, who could not forgive the slightest failure in culinary art, whose prodigiously refined taste would pounce upon a grain of super-fluous pepper, or the missing pinch of salt, whose extraordinarily developed taste-buds could trace by touch a few moments too many or too few of cooking, it must be admitted, we say, that the great Dodin dispatched to other stoves cooks whose talents many a gifted gourmet would justly have praised to the skies.

He needed perfection. How many times, during the long search which followed the death of Eugénie Chatagne, having methodically tasted and analysed a few mouthfuls of the dish proposed by the *cordon-bleu* undergoing the test, did he lay down his napkin and depart, without anger, to feed most honourably, certainly, but without glory, at the (to him) mediocre table of the Café de Saxe. He was resigned to the mediocrity of an eating-house. At home, he could not conceive of anything less than the absolute.

Dodin spent several bitter weeks in this manner. His house was haunted by short, fat women with scaly cheeks and childish eyes, crowned inharmoniously with scant, shiny hair tightly drawn back—by long, thin women bearing in the caverns of their cheeks the bitterness of involuntary virginity—by middling women, as insignificant as an aria from an Italian operetta, hatted in colourless straw, swamped by faded field-flowers. Not one allowed him, as she descended the porch steps, to hope for an unsuspected aptitude, as yet to be discovered and cultivated. His great soul grew heavy with melancholy. During this evil period, he indulged with less moderation than usual, but without abuse none the less, in that fresh and friendly claret which he whole-heartedly envied the cellar of the Café de Saxe, the only pride, if one were to take his word for it, of that establishment: a simple local wine, but of respectable age, from the best-favoured vine-yard, and ripened by the sun of a remarkable year, a wine which surprised the palate by its limpid simplicity, enchanted by its vaporous lightness, which slid supply, or rather insinuated itself into the throat, and which, from the depths of the stomach, still scented the lips with a perfume of crushed mulberries.

One September Sunday the charwoman opened the door and informed Dodin, with a strange smile, that 'a person was waiting for him in the drawing-room'. In a resigned and sceptical manner, Dodin entered his library and asked that she be shown in.

A disturbing creature crossed the threshold. In one look Dodin, as a connoisseur, had made out under the vulgar, somewhat worn, flowered dimity all the firmness of body, especially the breasts, of a well-rounded woman. In a face of charming lines, innocent and submissive eyes released a flood of caresses from beneath long eye-lashes soaked in shadow. She was hatless; untidy wisps of blonde hair, full of delicate lights, framed aesthetically, without overpowering it, a forehead not lacking in wit. The girl's decent and modest demeanour suggested one of those lives far removed from the gallant turmoil which sometimes pounces, the day's toil over, upon the escapees of the pantry and the stove; one of those lives undoubtedly devoted entirely to the domestic and clandestine happiness of employers whose passions are calm, intimate and ancillary: retired colonels, thrifty shopkeepers, or inexperienced undergraduates. The wise housewife who admitted this siren of the stove to her domain would have been certain of devoted service, and of keeping her husband at home.

Dodin, for the preliminary interrogation, drew his chair a trifle closer than usual to that in which he had installed the candidate. He rubbed the knees of his trousers energetically with his palms, as if to provoke a magnetic phenomenon which might prevent their getting lost. Finally, however, and more prudently, he dug his hands into his pockets. To tell the truth, during this conversation and most exceptionally, the calf-bound Grimod de la Reynière remained forgotten upon the shelf. Dodin had no thought, in order to fetch it, to leave the chair which had quite remarkably, he knew not how, moved yet nearer to that occupied by the pretty girl. The first interview, alas, revealed to the master of the house a bottomless and definite culinary incompetence, most mediocre dispositions, and practically non-existent experience.

Anyone else would have been eliminated at once. He had packed off to their soup kitchens without the slightest compunction, volunteers indubitably better qualified and wiser than this Agnes of the kitchen, but upon whom celestial graces had not been scattered with the same profusion. Dodin wished to hope against all hope. From one moment to the next he awaited the spark which would allow him at last to reconcile in one magnificent synthesis the obligations of his art and the satisfaction of his desire. And, in order to let this stroke of lightning rip through the dull, dark sky, to give the miracle a chance to occur, to provoke it, he lavished at length upon the timid and hopeless beginner the honours of the dining-room and the kitchen, slyly plotting the doorways so as to use them for apparently accidental collisions. However, he felt that in the ardent heat of these physical contacts, the whole nobility of his ideal suffered a deplorable abasement and approached the shame of capitulation. Stating boldly, who knows with what hopes, that a servant should be acquainted with the places in which she is to serve, he showed her the guest-room and the bathroom, and, relying upon some unexpected event, some sudden urge, he even led her into his own bedroom where Eugénie Chatagne's ghost troubled him not at all. During this visit the young girl displayed only a rather glum resignation which would no doubt have acceded promptly to any clearly expressed wish of her future master, but devoid of all provocativeness. Dodin, purple in the face, swept by a flood of desires, surreptitiously sketching with greedy hands immediately curtailed amorous gestures, was only protected (and that a most fragile protection) by the awareness of his mission and the obligations of his fame. To possess this girl was to sign an irrevocable contract, it was the abandonment of his reputation to the unschooled hands and uninspired soul of an apprentice incapable, alas, of any improvement. It was to hurl the art resurrected and defended by himself—Dodin-Bouffant—into the basest decrepitude, the lowest compromises, it was to decline, via filthy stews and vile hashes, to the shameful vulgarities of mere food. The master, then, was heroic—but of a somewhat craven heroism. To all appearances, and without the slightest illusion upon which to hang his hopes, this magnificent creature deserved to rank only among the most pitiable sauce-spoilers he had examined. He had unhesitatingly evicted others of whom he could have expected far more. But, to prolong her presence which occasioned in him an excitement not entirely imaginative, he proceeded with the usual interrogation as if he had not yet made up his mind, prolonging and complicating it, and trying with a supreme modesty, as much as was in his power, to steer his words away from the salacious paths where they kept straying.

Finally, having exhausted all oratorial artifices, he added:

'It is absolutely necessary, my child, for you to give me some practical demonstration of what you can do. I have three fine trout, fished this morning, a pretty spring chicken, and some celeriac. Prepare my evening meal. I shall have it at seven.'

Dodin spent a troubled day. He took his persistent desire to the Café de Saxe where he lost a game of chess without thinking about it; he went for a walk by the fresh river waters. In vain did he try to clear his thoughts of libidinous images; the longing for voluptuous embraces obstinately occupied a mind in which art, pure, chaste and noble, retained a foothold with the greatest difficulty. Sometimes, however, the dazzling glories of ancient French cookery passed and repassed before his eyes in confusion: torn standards in the centre of a violent storm; the goal, the sense, the grandeur of his life, in the dark surroundings where desire held him down, rose up in the full light, the glare of long flashes of lightning. Saint Anthony knew this anguish of blood. And, in his overheated imagination, the names, the faces of the great chefs, the famous gourmets, his peers, mingled heart-breakingly with his post-prandial plans of love.

Dodin sat down to dinner with the certainty that he was going to eat a detestable meal, but with the contrary belief that the so long awaited miracle had at last come to pass and that he would have a revelation. He hardly dared lift his gaze to the tragic aspect of the trout being served, slumped upon a silver dish. The nameless sauce in which they soaked indiscriminately, moved him to despair. The first mouthful timidly taken from a fillet which could have been magnificent routed his final hopes. In vain did he search in the mashed-up and odiously-boiled heads for the delicate cheeks of those river-partridges which he adored above all. Moreover, little by little, an odour of ill-cooked butter and half-raw shallots rose from the dish, settled in the room and made the gourmet's gorge rise. He could no longer conceal from himself the fact that the beautiful river-beast was ruined and massacred.

The loose and wrinkled skin of the succulent young chicken allowed him to dispense with tasting this dishonoured fowl.

He laid his napkin upon his dismal and useless bread, but, having reached the point of ultimate transactions with his conscience, did not for a moment consider going out to the Café de Saxe. She was there, quite near him, in the kitchen. He opened the door of his library. As he went in, he felt a surge of rebellion. After all, was he not free of his own life? If it pleased him to content himself with inglorious food, nobody was entitled to reproach him for taking into his home a graceful creature. From this very evening he would keep her and make of her his love whose awful fare he would accept knowingly and in full independence. And to plead his cause before posterity, he still had a long past of triumphs, of unforgettable culinary initiative, of uncontested mastery, which gave him the right to arrange his last years to suit himself, in his own way. But then his mouth filled with a savour of burned gristle, of gritty vegetables and charred meat; through the fever of Venus which throbbed at his temples, he half-saw the town, the region, the whole of France sitting down, through his fault, to shameful and sickening victuals; he convinced himself that his desertion must entail the collapse of those old traditions he had resurrected and made glorious. He felt upon him all the weight of a fame which was already widespread, imposing upon him, without respite, the role of arbiter of taste. Art, the art to which he had consecrated his life and which he had rescued from ignominious depths, took on material and charming shapes to appeal to him in his delirium.

These calls of duty were followed by a too cruelly precise vision of his shuttered room, full of the intimacy of a winter evening, in the golden dew of lamplight. Nothing stirred any longer in the house or the street. The bed was open, laden with the kindly weight of a voluptuous eiderdown, and before him, near the tapestry slippers, the young girl disrobed, her warm and passionate flesh gleaming through the falling linen.

Dodin opened the door to summon the fatal skivvy who, in the already wrecked and ravaged kitchen, unconscious both of the disturbance created by her beauty and the horror of her cooking, was ingenuously helping herself to the choice portions of the fowl scorned by her prospective employer. He closed the door again.

Here were new effluvia reaching his nostrils, here were new flavours caressing his sensitive palate: in a dream, ineffable snipe offered their robust scent to his over-excited senses; the wonderful earth condensed its strong perfumes in adorable white truffles; a celestial roast, pink velvet, butter of tenderness, lay moist before his eyes, flooded with matchless gravy.

He would know these delights no more. He would pass on neither their tradition nor their splendour. . . .

Dodin-Bouffant, suddenly very calm, called her in and said: 'Decidedly, my girl, no. I need someone with more experience. Learn, study, work . . . Perhaps later . . . Leave me your address.'

3

The Fourth Apostle

D odin, who was wont to formulate any number of inflexible laws and judicious principles upon the art of cooking and eating, professed, among other things, that the outer circumstances surrounding a meal, however perfect in itself, deserve meticulous attention and delicate vigilance.

'A Leonardo da Vinci in an attic, or a Beethoven sonata in a grocery, would have the most attenuated charms for me,' he used to say. 'Beauty requires a setting which allows one to receive all the delights she is capable of giving, and which, so to speak, brings to light all the possibilities of joy she embodies.'

Dodin-Bouffant had organized his dining-room with this great thought in mind. In that room he had balanced lighting and decoration, temperature and comfort, so that those moments of life spent in there should be natural and easy, and lose that ubiquitous quality of strife constantly exhibited by the hostility of things: a chair refusing to allow the body to assume a comfortable position, the stifling heater corrupting all sensation, an odious wallpaper forcing itself upon the eye.

But the great man's first preoccupation had been with the choice of his guests. In this he had allowed himself to be guided by an intransigence akin to ferocity. Experience had taught him to admit to his table none but elect natures of a sincerity on a par with high erudition, whose capacity for feeling was as developed as their sense of taste. In his first hours of fame, in his youthful enthusiasm and the pride of his resurrected art, he had welcomed to the succulence of his cuisine all those who craved the honour of tasting it. How many unworthy and inept false gourmets and vile flatterers had he seen trooping into his home! He had concealed with difficulty his heartaches upon hearing admiring exclamations at dishes he considered deplorable, or, on the contrary, on observing absent-minded and lukewarm enthusiasms before works of art which he knew to be perfect and which raised him to heights his guests were incapable of reaching. He had drunk to the dregs the flow of banalities and pretentious incompetence. His judgement of men grew more severe; gradually, he reduced the number of his companions. He had decided, before admitting them to his epicurean intimacy, secretly to submit them to pitiless tests, and, as he embarked with them in the dining-room or the library upon theoretical or practical culinary discussions, in the Supreme Court of his own science, he judged without their knowledge those heathens and those bad artists whose heresies, whose coarse tastes or whose superficial refinement debarred them, with no possible appeal, from the delights of the incomparable table.

The wealthy Bobage was not invited again after having taken for a Beaujolais an impeccable Châteauneuf-du-Pape.

Capada, the architect, was permanently ostracized for not

having recognized in the cream of a cauliflower sauce the exotic caress of a pinch of nutmeg.

A treasury official, having declared he could see no difference between a roast of Nivernais or of Franche-Comté beef, was struck from the visiting list.

Rigaille, manager of the local glass-works, committed one upon the other at the end of a meal two heresies which condemned him to exile: he emptied a glass of Pommard after a coffee-cake, and refused a perfectly marbled and brittle *persillé*.

Others suffered a similar fate for not having discerned the superfluous pinch of salt in a purée of cardoons, or for having unrestrainedly praised the badly buttered toast under a partridge of the wrong age.

Month by month, week by week, for many years Dodin-Bouffant had thus maintained a reign of terror and proscription over his contemporaries, compatriots or travellers, familiars or visitors, all seeking avidly to approach a glory which was becoming national, and to taste works of art all of whose subtleties they were incapable of appreciating, but whose charm and prestige impressed them.

Dodin had developed an implacable soul in his dealings with men. At the conclusion of these tests only three of the elect remained with him, three who had victoriously surmounted the innumerable obstacles and traps he had set for them, and whom he judged worthy of permanent admission to the felicities of his illustrious board. His dining-room was thenceforward closed to all others.

Surrounded by his faithful few, the artist no longer wished to try new experiments. He held that meals could only be enjoyed by a small number of guests, solidly united by a single ideal, and freed from the prejudices of politeness, convention, and affability imposed by the presence of a stranger.

Dodin was deaf to all appeals. Rich Americans, Russian princes, English lords, who, changing horses in Dodin's town, stayed on in the vain hope of an invitation, or who were taking the waters at the county spa, attempted without success to use official influence, personal contacts, direct and humble advances. They reaped nothing but disappointments.

The famous *gastronome* even gave his reasons for refusal to a German baron of the diplomatic world who was more pressing than the other supplicants, by explaining to him that 'he belonged to a country where it was not even suspected that anything other than *food* could pass one's lips'.

The Deputy Prefect himself, a jovial man of generous proportions and a remarkable trencherman, vainly juggled with flattery, promises and threats: he did not obtain access to the charmed circle. Courteously, Dodin sent him a cold shrimp pâté to thank him for instructing a forester to show him a nest of morels (a device designed to soften him). He also condescended to compose his menu on an occasion when the functionary was to entertain a Minister on tour. He thus contributed greatly to his promotion, but never bade him to his sanctuary.

Oddly enough, this rigid isolation and intransigent attitude aroused no hostility, at least locally, towards the sovereign of the table. The gourmet was cherished, raised to universal glory, for having been born and having stayed in the town, and for having attracted some of Fame's lustre to a city utterly devoid, until his day, of a Great Man; in a vague way the population was aware of its real inferiority beside such an artist.

Although the possibility had never crossed his mind, Dodin-Bouffant's prestige had gained by his retirement and his mystery.

He became the object of a more general and deeper respect, acquired an almost religious authority, a respect and authority which were shared, moreover, by his three friends who were regularly admitted to celebrate with him the cult of an art whose mysteries they had been able to pierce.

Passers-by looked at the shuttered house in the Rue de la Fontaine du Roi in which were elaborated the masterpieces discussed in the town and in the whole of France; and where hours were spent which everyone, without having shared them, declared to be unforgettable. Strangers were shown its modest grey porch and green shutters as they were shown the Café de Saxe, the pretty regency town hall, and the church (a ridiculous rococo edifice with a beautiful but incongruous romanesque portal).

And finally it must be said that Dodin-Bouffant's passion had fired the town with noble emulation.

Some, obscurely sensing through the mists of their ignorance, the magnitude of his achievement, and vaguely suspecting in the great compatriot's passion the existence of an inexhaustible source of perfect joys, had begun to introduce new refinements to their intimate tables. Others, impelled by base jealousy, wanted to prove that fine meals could be eaten elsewhere than at Dodin-Bouffant's; others yet had quickly assessed the possible profits to be derived from his renown, and realized that the illustrious gourmet's home town must attract strangers on the grounds of his fame. Thus a great number of small culinary circles had sprung up, and the town inns had noticeably raised their standards which were already most honourable. In this tiny Jura city, French cookery was in full renaissance under the great man's influence.

Needless to say, Beaubois the notary, Magot the cattle-dealer, and Doctor Rabaz, for long years Dodin-Bouffant's assiduous and faithful table companions, his only initiated disciples, the victors of the diabolical trials invented by the epicure determined to surround himself with experts, were also the only ones worthy of the master in every way, if not in creative genius, at least in their acute faculties of enjoyment and appreciation.

These, however, are the extraordinary circumstances in which Trifouille, the municipal librarian, became admissible to sit weekly in one of those vast wicker armchairs especially designed for the occupant's proper enjoyment and comfortable digestion, in which until then only three apostles had been invited to ensconce their vast rotundities.

One winter's evening, as Beaubois, Rabaz and Magot, relaxed and jovial, prepared themselves for a fricassee of large ceps in Château Yquem, by marinating in a golden sherry gullets already slightly overwhelmed by a hot and highly-seasoned pâté of pheasant-breasts, there was a violent ring at the front door. A panting man came in, solemnly bearing a carefully-covered china dish.

'Monsieur Dodin, I implore you,' said Bouringue, the bailiff, 'take me into your dining-room at once so that . . .' and as far as his precious burden would permit, he sketched the gesture of the Marathon runner, 'this dish may not grow cold; I have brought it running. I assure you that I have here, in my hands, happiness. When, just now at Trifouille's table, my lips touched this incomparable thing, it seemed to me suddenly that it would be celebrating the Holy Mysteries without the priest not to offer you this prodigious invention of Trifouille's. For he invented before my very eyes these inexpressible delights. . . .'

Bouringue had to be very certain of his facts to face the heavy, irate look of Dodin without flinching. Dodin was generous, and gave willingly, he was indulgent and forgiving to the grave or petty failings of human nature. But he remorselessly willed the swift demise of whoever dared disturb him when he was, so to speak, at the altar of his table.

However, shaken by Bouringue's inspired air, and overcome by his flood of admiring adjectives, he preceded him, almost in spite of himself, to the room where his anxious friends waited in the soft and friendly lamplight.

Silent and frowning he watched the bold intruder unwrap his dish. Suddenly, when the last rampart had fallen, the sanctuary was abruptly invaded by an intoxicating gust in which played, like naiads chasing each other in the waves, overtaking each other, brushing against each other, and then rolling over, all the freshness of succulent butters mingled with the rough and earthy scent of an incontrovertible Pouilly, the whole enhanced by a deep tidal odour, disturbing and bracing as an ocean wind. And the creation appeared, still smoking, upon the plates where it was portioned out. Two slices of firm, dense flesh whose admirable whiteness was lightly veiled by a trickle of amber butter, two slices separated from each other by a thick roll of stuffing whose warm, rosy, transparent colour suggested that it was kneaded from an old Burgundy, solidified by some miracle.

Dodin's face, suddenly relaxed, had taken on a solemn and absorbed expression of exaltation. His dilated nostrils inhaled the heady culinary incense. Bouringue, having accomplished his sacred mission, was rather at a loss: deeply moved, he stammered, and having, in a moment of inspiration, found the eloquence of enthusiasm and the power of persuasion, now no longer knew what to say or what to do with his hands.

Dodin-Bouffant, setting aside politeness as superfluous in

47

those solemn hours where one's being is moved to its profoundest reasons for living, drew to himself one of the plates in which, steaming, was the source of the divine aroma. He planted a determined fork into the very centre of the sumptuous piece, cut off a large portion, and having placed it in his mouth, closed his eyes and leaned back in his chair. And rejoiced! He savoured what his needle-sharp taste revealed to him at once: the two slices of lobster-meat simultaneously separated and united by a stuffing in which he could clearly distinguish the mildness of the new meat of a very young sucking-pig, emphasized by shallot and seasoning, strengthened by a touch of morel, blended with brioche dough, and indubitably blessed by a light aspersion of Burgundy.

When he reopened his eyes it was to fix upon Bouringue the indefinable gaze of an astronomer quitting the eyepiece of an instrument through which he has at last identified an unknown and passionately-sought planet, and he allowed these simple words to fall from his lips:

'Go and bring Trifouille to me.'

And while Bouringue, confusedly aware that he had just done a great deed and marked a historical date, went out dazedly, Dodin-Bouffant, showing his friends the enchanting dish with a sweeping gesture, said:

'Taste, O my dear comrades! We have perhaps found a man of genius.' And his full lips and white mutton-chop whiskers trembled with emotion.

When Trifouille appeared, pot-bellied, with small fiery wrinkled eyes in a plump, clean-shaven face, Dodin had given the cook his orders: he had had a new and clean cover laid in the place of honour—his own.

He awaited the author of the delectable dish upon the threshold.

'Trifouille,' he said majestically, 'swear to me that you are indeed the author of those lobster *bouchées*, that it is you, and you alone, who conceived them, prepared them, made them . . . swear to me, Trifouille!'

Stammering, scarlet with joy, drunk with glory, under the curious gaze of Bouringue who, his part played, contented himself with casting an eye dilated with admiration through the half-open door, Trifouille, the man who had just wrenched a cry of enthusiasm from the Napoleon of the culinary art, took a mumbled oath. Then Dodin-Bouffant, taking him ceremoniously by the hand, led him to the head of the table and, to his friends whose eyes were full of gratitude for the genial, intuitive, and perhaps unconscious inventor, he spoke these words which he had not pronounced for ten years, since Beaubois' solemn admission :

'Gentlemen, Monsieur Trifouille, the librarian, is henceforth one of us. He is worthy of admission to our circle. The creator of the admirable hors d'oeuvre which you have just tasted is a master, and I should be humiliated to celebrate without him the sacred cult to which we have consecrated our lives.'

Trifouille being in the president's seat, it was upon his plate that was placed the first pâté à la Choisy, which is made, as everyone knows, of boned partridges stuffed with their own pounded carcasses and livers, truffles, bacon-crumbs, and ordinary spices, these partridges being wrapped in drained and parboiled fat goose-livers, larded with fresh anchovies, which have been cooked in a light pastry, the last part of the cooking-time being baptized by half a glass of old eau de vie. This more than honourable course, a legacy of old French cookery, is only at its best with an aged, half-heady Saint-Gilles wine, endowed by the years with a generosity which is never the attribute of youth, with a temperate warmth already tinged with twilight.

49

4

Dodin-Bouffant Boiled Beef and His Royal Highness

Although his vanity was entirely unaffected by it, Dodin's fame had overstepped the boundaries of his province and even the frontiers of his country. The heavy mail delivered to him weekly by the Messageries postal services, as also the curiosity of travellers passing through the modest and peaceful city where the great man's existence flowed peacefully on, bore witness to the extent of his empire and the immensity of his renown. However, he shunned equally correspondents and visitors. He remained unpretentious, kindly, simple; devoting with ever more conscientious gravity and more concentrated ardour, the powers and meditations of his riper years to the subtle and

magnificent art to which he considered he owed, for the traditional glory of his country, the best of himself and the whole of
his active genius.

To his intimates, gathered around the lamp, after having read
aloud some pages of the old masters which restored to cookery
and the beauties of the table their true nobility, he would confess
his secret ambitions:

'The art of taste,' he would say, 'has so far only known untidy
and overgrown centuries, full of inventions and fine things,
certainly, rich and flavourful, abundant, even prodigal, but
tumultuous, devoid of rules and laws, bearing the stamp of
exuberant and somewhat confused youth. The table still awaits
its great classical century. There have been noble precursors,
but the kitchen has yet to see the birth of its Pascal and Molière,
its Racine and Boileau, geniuses of law and method, profound
and penetrating, great masters of tone and nuance, of oppositions
of light and shade, subtlety and enchantment, teachers and
arbiters of our palates, creators of our future laws. There is no
doubt that this fine flower of genius will be French. All, in
culinary history, indicates that our country is destined for the
honour of watching her soil produce the full blossoming of an
art which will take its undisputed place among the other great
arts. You are younger than I, my friends; modestly I have tried
to show you the way; meditate, work—you have on earth the
prodigious good fortune to inhabit the land, the only land,
perhaps, in which all the materials for erecting the edifice are to
hand, together. Yes, meditate, train your imagination to
combine flavours—hypothesis is the mother of all great discoveries; sharpen your faculties of taste. . . .'

One day the twice-weekly newspaper of that province, *The
Charter*, announced in its 'regional echoes' the arrival at the

waters of D. . . . of the heir to the throne of Eurasia. Rabaz read this item of news to Dodin, towards midday. The gourmet, in casual summer wear, lay back in a large wicker armchair at the edge of the lawn in his discreet and shady little garden, where a tired gaze rising over the chestnut tree, could rest upon the blue undulations of the Jura. He was sipping a cherry wine made with cinnamon and coriander, while the doctor punctuated his reading with large draughts of that royal velvety elixir which M. Bouscarat, distiller at Clermont-Ferrand, had just launched to replace the liqueur de Garus. The peaceful silence of August noontides lay upon the two drinkers.

Dodin did not appear to pay much attention to the arrival of the illustrious prince in the neighbourhood.

At the cook's invitation, they went to table. The half-darkened room was fresh, a trifle mysterious, and very comfortable. The two friends' menu, that day, was of the simplest. The entrée consisted of a white fish-*boudin*, which is made of eel, carp and pike, finely hashed with white breadcrumbs soaked in milk, the whole creamed with half a pound of fine fresh butter, heightened with delicate herbs and spices, yolks and whites of egg, and half a jug of cream. After blanching over a gentle fire it is placed in a fine skin and slowly recooked between two tins. There were also fried shrimps. After this, appetites were concentrated upon a joint of mutton, 'hedgehog' style, followed by a pâté of ox-tongue, and the asparagus ragoût with peas gently paved the way for the pear tart with ice-cream and orange-blossom biscuits. Modest wines, too: a witty and fresh Arbois with the entrées, a graceful Saint-Péray, more serious, with the main courses, a thoroughly Béarnais Jurançon with the vegetables, and a finger of very Spanish Rancio to sustain the sweetness of the pastries.

It was not until the asparagus that Dodin-Bouffant returned to the information in *The Charter*.

'This Prince of Eurasia,' he said, as if continuing to pursue aloud an earlier train of thought, 'is, they say, an amiable Highness. I have heard it said that, for a man of such rank, his table is most honourable and that he will not be satisfied by any but delicate, abundant, and skilfully concocted fare.'

The doctor was no little suprised at this praise, which his famous friend was usually so chary of dispensing.

They were nursing their digestions in Dodin's library with boiling coffee and lemon-and-nut ratafias, when the rhythmic trot of two well-matched horses stopped dead before the little front porch.

At the first knock Adèle went to open, and, having announced the visitor and received the master's acquiescence, showed in a clean-shaven gentleman in striped nankeen pipe-stem trousers and a double-breasted coat from which emerged a fluted neck-cloth. His hair was brushed upwards and forwards in the 'romantic' style, and his gestures were the acme of graceful ease.

'My master, the Prince of Eurasia,' he said, bowing, 'has sent me to you, Sir, to ask you and your suite to dinner. His Highness is not unaware of the boldness of his invitation. As a passionate admirer of your exquisite artistry, he knows, from the accounts of your life to which he listens eagerly, the degree of meditative seclusion you insist on and the justifiable distrust of strange tables which you entertain. His Highness dares to hope that you will make an exception in his favour, considering that he is wholeheartedly your disciple; that, without pretensions to your genius, he has devoted to the art of which you are the Master a great part of his existence; that he tries sincerely to live according to your principles, and that, not having yet, alas, succeeded in concentrating all his enthusiasm upon the single object of eating well, he has, however, attained the high level of belief that perfection in the art which you adorn is as serious a matter as the proper administration of his States. His Highness, with you in mind, has sent for his second Master of the Kitchens, the first being seriously ill with a malignant fever. He will arrive by tomorrow's stage-coach to collaborate with the Chef especially employed, at His Highness' request, by the Hotel, in order to serve you.'

Rabaz anticipated a courteous refusal. But the charm of the compliment had seduced Dodin in his most deeply hidden vanity, and, I should say, his noblest. It pleased him that a prince from distant lands should pay him homage and admit himself the son of his, Dodin's, effort and thought. Moreover, did not the envoy bring, in the warmth of the invitation, the delicate and flattering renown of the heir of Eurasia who had a great reputation as a refined connoisseur; did not that constitute for the *gastronome* a guarantee that he was not demeaning himself? A chef was coming on his behalf from the remotest depths of Europe. A prince sent him an ambassador with respectful compliments, a prince reputed for the sureness of his taste, the luxury of his table, his regard for sumptuousness in the thousand details which surround a banquet. And did not the Prince owe it to the glory of his guest, and to his own, to invite him only to a reception which would almost be an apotheosis?

Dodin-Bouffant accepted and designated Rabaz as his 'suite'.

On the appointed day, brilliant sunshine flooded the country-side with luminous joy, and scented it with the perfume of over-heated crops. An open carriage came to fetch the Prince's guests. Dodin-Bouffant was simply dressed in a black coat of

French cut, knee breeches, silk stockings, and buckled shoes. He carried his sword at the hip. Rabaz's waist was tightly hugged by a nigger-brown redingote, with a double collar; with this he wore white trousers and a long-furred silk felt hat.

The journey was enchanting. The blue mountain in the tepid mist seemed very distant. The cattle, already lying down in the cool meadows, were chewing the cud of sweet-smelling grasses. Village thatches dripped with light and gaiety, even the shadows of the trees were impregnated with brilliance. There was joy at every turn of the road. Partridges ruffled the cornfields in their crazy race, like a breeze skimming the earth, and Dodin, pointing to a hare diving between a cow's muddy legs, beside the grey and tumbledown stones of a little vineyard wall, exclaimed: 'What admirable country! Look, Rabaz, at that marvellous combination: the creature, the cream, the wine: a complete jugged hare!'

As they passed a pond, half-hidden under a vault of trees, water-insects surrounded them in buzzing flight and all the life of summer sang in their iridescent wings.

The Master of Ceremonies awaited them in the great court-yard. He helped the Master and his 'suite' to descend from the dusty carriage and led them to the Prince who most graciously bade them be seated. They were soon released from the prim solemnity of introductions. They were offered vermouth, fresh cream of absinthe with cinnamon, and frosted *cédrat* liqueur. Dodin maintained a dignified reserve, occasionally emitting in measured tones aphorisms which, when he managed to pierce their depths, drew from the Prince glances full of admiration.

Then the meal was announced. The table was laid with discreet good taste. China and setting were of a tender blue shade which was restful to the eye without appealing to it too much, nor distracting it from its true occupation which must be contemplation of the dishes.

'Master,' said the Prince, addressing his guest, 'I am not among those who believe that the details of a banquet should be elicited from pasteboard, out of the corner of one's eye, surreptitiously and almost shamefully. Permit, therefore, without imputing to it an ostentation of which my intentions are innocent, that my Master of Ceremonies should read aloud to you the modest meal which he will have the honour of serving.'

The guests, in a pensive attitude, listened.

'Please announce, Master of Ceremonies,' ordered the Prince.

His hand on the pommel of his sword, the officer began in a loud and severe voice:

'The soups will be:

One of Pigeon Bisque

One of Quail in Coulis *à la Reine*

One of Shrimp

And the other of Stuffed Soles.

For the centre-dish, a Yearling Boar.

At either end a Royal Pâté and a Pheasant Pie with Green Truffles.

The Hors d'Oeuvres will be:

One of Spitted Partridges with Herbs and Essence of Ham

A *Poupetin* of Turtledoves

Two of Sausage *à la Dauphine*

One of Stuffed Pike.

The main Entrée will consist of:

Two Stuffed Chickens in Cream

Young Rabbits *a la Saingaraz*

River-Birds garnished with Oysters.

And the wines of this first course will be: After the soup, dry

Sherry, and for the white: a Carbonnieux, a Langon, a Meursault and a Pouilly. For the red: some la Chainette, Thorins, and Saint Estèphe. And whilst the second service is being laid, Cyprus Malvoisie and Madeira will be served.'

The officer bowed, saluting with a flourish of his cocked hat upon which flowered a mauve and gold cockade, the colours of the House. He continued:

'The second course will be of two *relevés* preceding the four great roast dishes:

One of *Lottes à la Vestale* from the Lake of Geneva and the other of Torrent Trout *à la Chartreuse*. The roasts will be:

Turkeys *à la Daube*
Ribs of Beef Hollandaise
Breast of Veal *au Pontife*, accompanied by
Sweetbreads in the same fashion and Dumplings
from the same cuts
And a Leg of Mutton in Stuffed Fillets.

There will be four sauces:

Piquante
Poor Man's Sauce
Sky Blue
And *à la nichon*.

And three salads:

Of Herbs
Of Oranges
And of Olives.

The hot side-dishes of this course, to escort the Roasts and Salads, will be:

Of Stuffed *Chanterelle* Mushrooms
Of Cockscombs in 'Pagodas' in Champagne Wine
Of Asparagus

Of *Rôties en Rocher*

Of Carps' Roes in Béchamel Sauce

And of Truffles *à la Maréchale*.

The wines of this course will be, for the white: Haut-Preignac, Muscat de Frontignan, Jurançon and Seyssel; for the red: Côte St. Jacques, Cortaillod-en-Neuchâtel, Richebourg and and Romanée-Conti.

And whilst the third course is being prepared, the following will be served:

Maraschino Ices

Tokay, Grenache and Lachryma Christi Wines.'

The officer again bared his head to bow. He continued:

'The third course will be, for the soups:

One of Minced Chicken Whites

One of Clear Stock

And one *Ouille au Bain Marie*.

For the Entrées:

Hure of Salmon

Rabbits *Père Douillet*

Goose *à la Carmagnole*

Larks *au Gratin*

Pheasant in Gondolas

Terrine of Snipe.

For the hors d'oeuvres, accompanying the entrées:

Fish Sausages

Blanc-Manger Fritters

Foie Gras *à la Cendre*.

The desserts will be:

Of four plates of fruit stews, pastries and jams:

Quince Stew in Scarlet Jelly

Grilled Peach Stew

Nut Paste

Violet Jam.

There will be:

Sweet Oranges and Pears in Liqueur

Cinnamon and Jonquil Candies

Griddle Cakes with Spanish Wine

Cornets and *Gimblettes*

Marzipan 'Love Lakes'

Macaroon Trifle

Ices of Rose, *Epine-vinette*, and Grenadine

Almond Pastries

Iced Cheeses

And refreshing Fennel, Pistachio and Almond Essences.

'The wines of this course will be, for the white: Yvorne, Rochecorbon, Puy-Notre-Dame and Vouvray; for the red: Chambertin, Mouton-Lafitte, Hermitage and Lunel. They will be followed by the red Champagnes of Bouzy, of Verzenay and of Porto.

Moka Coffee. White Ratafias of Grenoble Apricots,

Muscatels and Aniseed.'

Dodin-Bouffant did not listen to this opulent menu without some occasional wrinkling of his olympian brow. Not that he was moved by the number of dishes. He was one of those men whose delicacy of manner and gesture, whose lightness of touch, whose distinction at table have so much charm that they conceal the extent of their appetite. This gourmet feared no menu, should it keep him at table a day and a night, but he knew how to relish it with a grace which caused his fantastic capacity to be over-looked. Whatever the abundance of the table he faced it in fine fettle, but so elegantly that he appeared but to nibble. Dodin, unafraid, felt perfectly capable of standing up to even more gargantuan repasts. But, in passing, he had noticed certain shocking solecisms in the composition of dishes and the order of succession of flavours—solecisms undoubtedly due more to a desire to shine than to a sincere search for harmony.

For instance, as centre dishes, to the wild boar he would have preferred river-veal *en daube* with pistachios, as the right-hand pâté was Royal and the left-hand pie of pheasants; an accumulation of heating meats of opposing flavours which paired, unfortunately for this special course, two kinds of game which cannot succeed each other in any order. Then again, in the first hors d'oeuvres, he disapproved of stifling the suavity of partridges under essence of ham, just as he found it difficult to accept the conclusion of the second roast being a leg of mutton, after white breast of fowl which in any case, to ensure a proper transition, he would have liked marinated rather than *à la Pontife*. He was also greatly shocked to find a fresh Cortaillod between the generous warmth of a Côte St. Jacques, a Richebourg and a Romanée.

The meal proceeded according to the menu, with certain errors, however, in the order of the wines, their suitability for the dishes they accompanied, and the choice of year. There is no doubt, as Dodin later explained to Rabaz, that the 1817 Saint Estèphe, less violent, more attenuated, would have been more appropriate than the 1819 to the somewhat pallid flavour of the cream stuffing in the two chickens of the first course.

Dodin further noticed that the dough, the texture and the baking-time of the breads served had suffered from a total lack of care and discernment in their selection to accompany each dish, for it is not a matter of indifference haphazardly to offer crumb or crusty, brioche or Vienna loaf with any and every meat and vegetable.

The courses followed each other, and as pride spread over the Prince's features His Highness, undermined, no longer offering any but the feeblest resistance to the abundance of victuals and the copious draughts of liquid, so the face of the King of Gourmets grew severe, one might almost say critical. He was making an effort, for he was courteous, to conceal his disappointment under a good-humour which could not rise above indulgence, in other words, a humour insulting in spite of himself. The Master of Ceremonies, who began to look pinched and scornful, noticed the obvious: a total lack of sympathy was growing between the two Highnesses.

Rabaz, the product of too refined a schooling not to understand the situation, and moreover professionally accustomed to sounding the human heart, followed the successive stages of the Master's displeasure, wholeheartedly approving its rigour, but attempting, by a display of warmth and redoubled appetite, to attenuate the latent hositility. He was handicapped in this conciliatory task, and would have given half his practice to dare unbutton his coat.

Dodin ate conscientiously rather than with fervour, as a loyal man who wishes to carry the test to its ultimate conclusions and to judge only upon complete evidence. He ate without flinching, without fatigue, drinking unhesitatingly according to the dish from one or the other of the glasses before him which the wine-waiter automatically refilled. The number of dishes and wines could not impinge upon his perfect sang-froid which the Prince of Eurasia, more easily moved, envied him and admired sincerely.

The conversation was extremely slow as if, subjects being henceforward limited, it was feared that those which were still permissible and harmless might run out before the end of the meal.

61

The dessert appeared at last. His Highness, who assuredly, according to the customs of the great, had paid more attention to his own pleasure than to his guests', did not appear affected by the tepid reserve of Dodin-Bouffant. Delighted with the feast he was giving, he did not for a moment suppose that his companions were not dazzled; although still perfectly correct and master of himself, he had however reached that degree of bliss in which one is ready to interpret most favourably the doubts which spare no rank. It was the gentle hour when mortals of slight importance, their hunger satisfied and their thirst slaked, suddenly decide upon a definite conquest of glory, and when sovereigns inwardly resolve to rule through justice and mercy.

The cigars, brought at immense expense from the Islands in ingeniously ventilated boxes, exuded the scent of burning creole bodies; the ratafias and eaux-de-vie were above reproach, which conferred upon the final hour a little relaxation and abandon.

Dodin-Bouffant and his suite took their leave of the Prince with great courtesy, but the Master could not help wrapping his thanks in imperceptible *nuances* which proved that his honest heart was incapable of complete falsehood.

It was high time, moreover, for the carriage to turn out of the great alley of oaks which led from the villa reserved for the prince and his court. Dodin had an immediate pressing need to speak.

'What a pity, my poor Rabaz, to see so many gifts and precious elements wasted and ruined like that! Through this great lesson you have been enabled to confirm the truth of what I have so often declared to you. That poor fellow of a Prince—and Eurasia is fortunate in that he is one of the best—is still living in barbarous times. The work he set before us was abundant, thick-set, rich! But without light, without brilliance. No air, no logic, no line. Custom, but no rules. A parade, but no organization.

What mistakes in the succession of flavours and textures! Can one serve a quail soup after a pigeon bisque? And in two adjacent courses stuffed sole and stuffed pike? What can one say of a *gastronome*, or one who considers himself as such, who makes no call upon a large fish or tidal shell-fish, strong-scented and unexpected in this region? He brings a chef, and no lobster! And what a chef! who, haphazardly, with no concern for the taste and substance of meats, places a goose between rabbits and larks, and presents it *à la Carmagnole* when, in the same course, the palate has already undergone the violence of vinegar-impregnated sauces whereas it should have been kept cool in order to capture the delicate *nuances* of the snipe? Neither do I like the almond pastries, which demand so much attention and analysis, being served after the ices which paralyse and lull the faculties, and before the cheeses, also iced, which must therefore leave an aftertaste of vulgar pomade. As for the secondary wines, they were as badly distributed as possible, and in a most unfortunate ignorance of the gustatory preparations.

'These are already not minor errors. There are others which provoked me to such a state of rage, my friend, that I nearly allowed myself to create a regrettable scandal. That chef is a sorry wretch, and his master a man devoid of taste. I am sorry to say it of a prince who wished us well. But is it really permissible to stifle the divine perfume of nature under such sophisticated sauces? Under the hollandaise, for instance, could you detect the faintest trace of that healthy and energetic aroma of beef, moreover sadly selected from the scruff of an animal grazed, no doubt, in somewhat damp pastures? On the other hand, the banality of that hollandaise! I found it identically under the mask of the Béchamel and the Saingaraz. And that thick garnish *à la Vestale*, which so annoyingly concealed from me the scent of water-herbs which should predominate in the flesh of a *lotte*, that devil's cook had the temerity to try and make me appreciate it again in his chicken-breast *panade*, and in his *poupetin* of turtle-doves! Ah, Rabaz! That man is of the detestable breed of false artists who, on the morning of a feast, concoct three pots of sauce: one Spanish, one dark, and one white, and then scatter them into all their dishes, sharpened, thinned out, thickened, but without a thought for the superior laws, the matings, matchings, combinations, oppositions, chiaroscuros, lights and shades by which one enhances the very essence of the vegetable or animal, its intimate flavour, its essential character, whose deficiences one corrects, whose beauties one frames, and by which one brings out what is divine in it, the deepest and least recognized soul of its beings. Cuisine, that? Come, come—for Iroquois, for Princes, for Germans. Not for us.'

Dodin-Bouffant fell silent and Rabaz, caught up in these higher speculations, said nothing. Evening was already roving over the slopes of the Jura, under the trees, along the streams, and the dust of the day, put to flight by the imminent coolness, no longer left in the peaceful air more than wide swathes of bluish ash. The herds and flocks went tinkling towards the freshwater troughs. Women sat on farm thresholds. Summer wrapped itself in night.

'I shall teach that prince a lesson. I shall send him an invitation, Rabaz!' concluded Dodin.

Beaubois, Magot and Trifouille awaited the travellers in the Master's study. But he, ill-humoured, asked Rabaz to excuse him. He had served to him in his room, before retiring, simply a clear soup with a poached egg and a few wisps of tarragon, a turkey-breast in wine jelly, and a fricassee of asparagus tips. He dipped a few biscuits in a glass of Grenache, drank a great draught of honeyed lime-tea, threw Adèle a grateful look, and slipped into a cool bed where, however, he dreamed that a chef with a lugubrious quaker's face, dressed half as a cook and half as Lucifer, forcibly funnelled into him enormous saucepansful of thick sauce made with mineral essences and horrible chemical compounds.

In the town's only carriage (repainted, varnished and newly upholstered in dust-coloured repp for the occasion) Trifouille the librarian was dispatched on the appointed day to fetch the Prince. Dodin-Bouffant chose this way of informing His Highness that Rabaz was not the only member of his Household.

He allowed no one but himself to wash and prepare the china, an old Nyon set with tiny blue flowers, of such a smooth texture that knives slid upon its surface as on a pane of glass—a precious service which had belonged to his great-grandmother.

The illustrious *gastronome's* invitation had filled the Prince with emotion and delight. And, rather than miss this feast which was to crown him permanently among the world's great sovereigns, and conferred upon him, he believed, a nobility rare and more precious than his escutcheon, he would have dismissed his Council, or postponed his despatches until the next mail. He was almost tearful in his tender anticipation of the culinary triumphs with which the gourmet would regale him.

Dodin awaited him in the library, surrounded by Rabaz, Beaubois and Magot, all four in redingotes, but so dressed as to be able to confront the most gigantic banquet in perfect comfort and ease.

The introductions over—and the Heir of Eurasia could not help feeling at once that these universal masters of the table, these gods of the kitchen, were his equals in their science—the crowned guest was refreshed by an old Paphos, duly iced, some

Arbois with cloves at its peak of freshness, and Italian bitters tempered by strawberry and lemon essences, and then, without further delay, the company moved into the dining-room where the shade, in the dog-days, was quite heavenly and propitious to great spiritual experiences.

The table appointments, the porcelain and silver, the simple flowers negligently scattered over a fine and spotless cloth, conveyed a sense of harmonious peace compounded of dignity, cordiality and delicacy. When everyone was comfortably seated in those vast armchairs which he had designed with such care, Dodin rose and read from a piece of card the following:

'Menu of the meal offered by the President Dodin-Bouffant to His Royal Highness the Crown Prince of Eurasia.

Dainties before the Soup

Adèle Pidou's Soup

Brillat-Savarin's Fritters

Dodin-Bouffant's Boiled Beef garnished with its own Vegetables

Soubise Purée

Dessert

White Wines of the slopes of Dezalay and of Château-Grillé

Red Wines of Châteauneuf-du-Pape, of Ségur and of Chambolle.'

That was all. He sat down again. With the last word a cold, cruel embarrassment descended around the table where so many hopes and illusions had just crumbled. The guests no longer dared look at each other, and although the silence hung strangely heavy upon them, could find no words in their throats, choked as they were with disappointment.

The Prince, reflecting that this meagre programme would

hardly have provided the first course of his ordinary meals, wondered inwardly whether he should countenance having been brought from so far and disturbed in order to eat boiled beef which, at home, he left to the servants' hall.

Those four little dishes—that was all he would have to show for his reception by Dodin-Bouffant!

Trifouille, Rabaz and Beaubois oscillated between the terror of a battle-royal, and the disappointment of their belief that the day would be the apex of their ascension to the transcendental peaks of culinary intoxication. They were perfectly certain, though, that this frugal fare would be above reproach.

Dodin, his sensual, shaven lip puffed out by his efforts to conceal the smile which tickled it, sat down again serenely.

One of those moments pregnant with anxiety fluttered over everyone and everything—moments in which those who live through them long for the earth to open suddenly and swallow them up, or, conversely, for the heavens to fall, thus ending the torture of awaiting, second after second, the explosion of an august wrath.

Dodin rang, pressing down a copper owl's beak, and Adèle, with ridiculous little curtsies, bore in the tray burdened with dainties which she arranged upon the table, her clumsy gestures of politeness interspersed with irritable grunts. There were mushroom and shrimp jellies, tiny preserved trout stuffed with tarragon and chopped olives, fresh sausages from the village of Payerne, their fat and juicy meat scented with wood-essences, minced pigeons in cream, eggs stuffed with scented dumpling dough, buttered toast-fingers crowned with domes of pounded duck-livers, rissoles of melted cheese wrapped in spikelets of ham, minute cold boned thrushes, larded with layers of anchovy, small tubs of roes pricked with cloves and powdered with red pepper, cold lemon tunny-fish pilaffs, iced eels stuffed with pounded prawns, fried blood-sausages made of game and sausage-meat, and a graceful pat of well-moulded fresh butter.

The profusion and riches of these hors d'oeuvres meeting over-stimulated appetites certainly succeeded in attenuating the dreadful embarrassment which, uninvited, had sat down green and hollow-cheeked among the choice guests; but, even so, as they plunged doughty spoons into the dishes or attacked them with unhesitating forks, each of them heard resounding in his ears the vulgar, inglorious, grease-smelling sound of those two little words: 'Boiled Beef'.

The powerful jaw-movements of these men, trained to all the noble exercises of gastronomy, seemed veiled with regret, with distress, even with reproach. These chosen creatures, of whom four at least were no doubt the finest flower of the world's culinary intellect, ate heartily at this melancholy moment in their history—as much to guard against the slenderness of the following courses as to grow drunk (as a musician gets drunk on harmony, or a painter on colours) upon the prodigious symphony of flavours composed and blended with the superior and unfailing skill characteristic of the Master's creations. He played as a virtuoso upon all the shadings of that infinitely complex exaltation borne to the brain from the impressions of the palate, in turn gentle and brutal, amiable and grave, disturbing and warm. And the well-cooled Dézalay, with this piled-up prodigality of precious trifles, flowed smoothly down the throat, life-giving and scented, its aromatic freshness irrigating every taste-bud, bringing both repose and stimulus.

At this moment, then, the guests' feelings were extremely contradictory.

However, the unexpected and quintessential refinement of

Dodin's first course had prejudiced them favourably to welcome the soup. And Dodin knew it, as a great general who alone perceives the invisible instant when the battle is won.

This soup was quite simply a masterpiece. Very complex, of lengthy preparation, it had a slightly old-fashioned, Greuze-like charm; but also certain Ribéra brutalities, and some unforeseen Da Vinci tenderness. Broadly speaking it was reminiscent of a sonata's development, in which each theme retains its own life and its own individual flavour within the blended power and harmony of the whole. There was one single taste, but each part of this taste kept its own personal and natural quality. The basis was of two superimposed stocks, both very strong and concentrated, the one of a large skirt of beef, and the other of the juice of several pounds of fresh vegetables, cooked in a very little water to which a suspicion of liqueur Champagne had been added to give it body. To this quintessence a light mixture of mushroom and white asparagus in equal parts had been added; an alert palate could also distinguish a few cups of chicken broth in which several egg yolks with a generous dose of nutmeg had been beaten up for additional smoothness. Upon this divine and odoriferous liquid, like treasure islands, swam parboiled artichoke bottoms laden with a butter-fried stuffing in which carps' roes and mushrooms were mashed up together with cream; under the smoking surface, diving into the mirror-like depths, pearls heavy with beauty, were small rissoles of shrimp-tails laced in melted cheese.

This soup instantly won over everyone, and when the relieved five, lighter-hearted, attacked the Brillat-Savarin fritters, rapturous contentment descended upon them. This dish consisted of small round fritters, crisp enough to offer the tooth some slight resistance, that it might only a quarter of a second later reach the tender and creamy heart of the treasure. But then! . . . Of these tiny worlds, amber-skinned as a beautiful Sinhalese, some ingeniously concealed in their golden wrappings *lotte* livers barely tinged with butter, others, soft bone-marrow scented with saffron; there were some whose cherished secret was snipe-brains preserved in a marinade of Volnay. And finally, precious autumn cardoons burst from the rounded flanks of the burning-hot, delicious fritters.

The Prince of Eurasia, intoxicated by all these natural scents, not one of which was masked by a criminal sauce, but whose seasonings, on the contrary, were designed to emphasize their natural essential graces, the Prince of Eurasia, I repeat, began to understand. His wit was, moreover, urged on to these discoveries by a marvellous Châteauneuf-du-Pape which blew into the soul like a good ocean wind into a sail, all the sunshine it had stolen, all the fervour of that baked earth of the Rhone Valley, its spiritual mother-country, and which, in waves of enlaced tannin and raspberry, brought to the brain a marvellous lucidity.

Trifouille was grave, Rabaz thoughtful, Magot red, and Beaubois uplifted with enthusiasm. Their happiness would have been complete had they not awaited that damned Boiled Beef which could upset everything. The Prince, despite his stupe-faction before the discovery that in a region of the human mind where he had thought himself a past master he knew almost nothing, despite his delight in possessing, at that moment, so many incomparable masterpieces, still wondered inwardly (with a dignity very close, however, to capsizing before such artistic raptures) how to take the insult offered to his rank when the coarse lackeys' dish should appear. We must not conceal that with each attack upon the wonderful fritters he inclined more and more towards clemency.

It arrived at last, that fearsome boiled beef, scorned, reviled, insulting to the Prince and to all gastronomy, Dodin-Bouffant's boiled beef, prodigiously imposing, borne by Adèle upon an immensely long dish which the cordon bleu held so high aloft at arms' length, that at first the anxious guests could see nothing whatsoever. But when, cautiously and with purposeful slowness, it was placed upon the table there were several minutes of genuine astonishment. Each guest's return to self-possession was marked by personal rhythms and reactions. Rabaz and Magot mentally scourged themselves for having doubted the Master; Trifouille was seized with panic before the display of such genius; Beaubois trembled with emotion. As for the Prince of Eurasia, he wavered between the noble desire to create Dodin-Bouffant a Duke immediately, as Napoleon had wished to do for Corneille, a wild urge to offer the *gastronome* half his fortune and half his realm to take over the reins of his gustatory administration, the irritation of being taught a lesson which was now crystal clear, and his haste to cut into the marvel which laid before him its intoxicating promises.

The beef itself, lightly rubbed with saltpetre and then gone over with salt, was carved into slices of a flesh so fine that its mouth-melting texture could actually be seen. The aroma it gave forth was not only that of beef-juice smoking like incense, but the energetic smell of tarragon with which it was impregnated and the few, very few, cubes of transparent, immaculate bacon in the larding. The rather thick slices, their velvety quality guessed at by every lip, rested languidly upon a pillow made of a wide slice of sausage, coarsely chopped, in which the finest veal escorted pork, chopped herbs, thyme, chervil. . . . But this delicate triumph of pork-butchery, cooked in the same broth as the beef, was itself supported by ample cuts from the breast and

71

wing fillets of farm chickens, boiled in their own juice with a shin of veal, rubbed with mint and wild thyme. And, to prop up this triple and magnificent accumulation, behind the white flesh of the fowls (fed exclusively upon bread and milk), was the stout, robust support of a generous layer of fresh goose-liver simply cooked in Chambertin. The arrangement was repeated again, in the same alternating order, forming distinctly separate parts, each marked by a boundary of assorted vegetables cooked in the broth and then lightly warmed in butter; each guest was to extract, in one stroke, between spoon and fork, the quadruple enchantment which was his share.

Subtly, Dodin had reserved to the Chambolle the honour of escorting this dish for the elect. A 'plain' wine would have clashed with one or another of the ingredients; the Chambolle, a thing of *nuances*, complex and complete, had in its pinky-gold blood sufficient variety for the palate to select, at the right time, according to the meat impregnating it, the necessary tone, the indispensable note.

A profound psychologist, Dodin had calculated his effect to perfection; those refined souls tasted a double delight: freed from the black worry which had obsessed them, and exulting in their senses at the flowering of an unexpected masterpiece, the chains of anguish fell from them for good and all at that precise moment when the warmth and virtue of the wines inclined them to the full, free life. Congenial wholehearted enjoyment could now give itself free rein in that intimate atmosphere. No more shadows. They were reassured. They might abandon themselves, in all contentment, to the pleasures of taste, and to that sweet, confident friendship which beckons to well-born men after meals worthy of the name.

Certainly, the Prince had understood—but his honour was

safe. Better still, in the future he would have the pleasure of recounting the story in the most charming manner to the Queens of other Courts, his customary table-companions, and be able to swear, without fear of contradiction, that he had eaten the most prodigious boiled beef imaginable.

There did linger, in his royal soul, some bitterness from the lesson he had been given to which he was not insensible. Suddenly, by retrospective comparison, he realized the imperfections which had lain concealed beneath the apparent magnificence of the meal which he himself had ordered. He seemed once more to detect, disagreeably, the monotonous and standardized flavour of the three sauces parcelled out with each dish in each course. He felt that however rich, however powerful, however Royal a Highness he might be, the famous Dodin-Bouffant, spiritually, upon the very battlefield where he, the Prince of Eurasia, had challenged him to combat, had just triumphed over him and inflicted upon him an acid critique of his grandiloquent fare. It may well have been that, turning over these considerations in his head, considerations so galling to his vanity—now that, devoid of all its glory, the residue of the glorious dish was being removed—the noble guest was on the point of becoming embittered. However, he had not the time, suddenly gripped at the nostrils as he was by a pungency in which sang all the sweetness of the earth, a pungency at the same time mild and robust, distinct and yet infinitely varied. Like the nacreous, milky flesh of the onions whence it came.

Ah! that purée! The epicure allowed no one but himself to prepare it. Thirty-six hours in advance he would himself select, one by one, young onions, identical in size, colour and flavour. Slowly, he would cut them into equal slices, and then, in a wide, deep, earthenware pot, dispose those slices one by one in superimposed layers, and when he had completed three of these, between the last and the next, lay a magnificent thickness of very fine, very fresh butter. He ceased this meticulous work only a few centimetres from the rim of the vessel. He would then pour over the preparation half a bowl of excellent fresh clear broth, and a glass of liqueur Champagne—very old, very smooth, and above all free of any sugar-processing. Then, over the contents, he would seal the lid of the earthenware pot, to keep the concentrated perfume locked in. And for thirty-six hours, on a very gentle fire of oak branches, the dish cooked slowly, gravely, religiously. Dodin's regular table-companions knew this marvel. But the Prince, who until that day had considered as a varlets' treat the vulgar and much decried vegetable, was suddenly reconciled both to the root and to the Maréchal de Soubise whom he had formerly dubbed, for giving his name to this dish, 'a panderer to the rabble'.

With the coffee and liqueurs, His Highness, having thrown off all pomp, almost sprawling in a huge old armchair, chewing at a cigar of no elegance but of delicious flavour which Dodin imported from Switzerland, felt himself invaded by a beatific sense of being, for the first time, simply a completely happy man.

Dodin, perfectly content, had a half-smile. He triumphed. To the oh so vain culinary sumptuousness of the Prince he had replied by a meal which was simple, short, bourgeois, but whose profound art had convinced even the dispenser of superfluous luxury of his own unworthiness.

And as, by the open door of the carriage, the illustrious gourmet bowed before the vanquished, confounded, but delighted Prince, suddenly the latter, solemnly, held out his hand and said:

'From no one but you, dear host, could I have accepted the

lesson I have just been taught. Comfort my somewhat bruised vanity by giving me a single formula the secret your genius alone has discovered. Great cookery . . .?'

'Is a choice work which demands much love. . . .' answered Dodin-Bouffant with a deep bow.

5

Wherein Dodin-Bouffant Makes an End of It

'The Prince's Dinner' as they called it in the town once its details became known, was one of the triumphs of Dodin-Bouffant's career. Of course his four disciples did not hold their tongues for long: that very evening the Café de Saxe knew that the day had been a glorious one for the city—three days later the entire province shared their civic pride and the event was discussed in many inns, from the taverns of Geneva to the famous 'Golden Pike' at Lyon. The hero of the day took no pride in it other than that of having produced a masterpiece *ad majorem gastronomiae gloriam* and written a fine page in the history of the table. In his equitable soul, Dodin rendered to his cook the homage which was her due and loyally attributed to her a fair share of their success. The conceit, its direction, to a great extent the actual substance of the marvellous meal were his own

76

work, but Adèle Pidou, he admitted to himself, had been the incomparable handmaiden of his brain.

Adèle Pidou! The charm and the torment of the great man's existence! His main reason for living and his rack! It will be remembered that the death of Eugénie Chatagne was followed for Dodin, thenceforth deprived of that great artist, by a procession of aspirants to her awesome functions. During gloomy days, Dodin surveyed a series of faces devoid of any spark of genius, of any great passion, lifeless eyes adapted far more to following the flight of iridescent gadflies over muddy cow-flanks than to the contemplation of that moist gold which, little by little, colours the skin of fine fat birds, stuffed with butter and patiently basted. But suddenly, just as the desperate *gastronome* was seriously contemplating doffing the old magistrate's frock coat and replacing it by the white attire of a cook to ensure his own comfortable living and the delight of his friends, Adèle Pidou, last in the line, appeared upon his doorstep. Short, stocky, her round and jovial head lit up by canny eyes, haloed in a very clean but very worn calico kerchief, she placed upon the master's desk without ceremony her basket in which a squawking duck kicked at the fresh vegetables with its tied legs. Then, quite unembarrassed, she settled down in a comfortable armchair. Oh! Dodin had no need, to save them from the wanderings of temptation, to put his hands in his pockets. The fat thighs, overfull bodice, double chin and somewhat faded hair of his visitor imbued him with invincible respect. After a long conversation in which her ingenuous and unconscious but very sure taste soon became apparent to the psychologist, he took her, according to his customary ritual, but with marked consideration, to visit the dining-room and the kitchen. The cordon bleu's eye, with an odd gleam of interest and evident enthusiasm, pleasurably

77

caressed all the complicated and ingenious appointments. Dodin followed her gaze and dissected it with emotion. Indeed, just as a thoroughbred horse leaps forward into space, or as a writer quivers with impatience before a blank sheet of paper and a well-trimmed pen, so Adèle Pidou could not restrain herself; she began, for no reason at all save the pleasure of touching them, to seize the handles of frying-pans and skillets, of copper saucepans, to stroke the rounded flanks of the earthenware pots, to feel the bottles of spices, the boxes of ingredients, to open them, sniff them, examine the stove, inspect the spits and the fish-kettles. Dodin, throbbing with hope, allowed her to please herself. Perhaps, at last. . . . And, seated upon the chairs of the Temple they resumed a conversation already more intimate, more confiding.

'Yes,' said Adèle Pidou suddenly, 'don't know, but p'raps what I cooked up t'other day for our little Louis' christening might've pleased your Honour. There's my young brother, Jean-Marie, who'd poached a lovely "hairy"—a young hare, you know, but big already, 's'what they call a Capuchin. Well, for a change, and to give 'em a treat, I thought of soaking it in our own *marc*, that we distil ourselves, 'n then to bone it gently when it'd taken properly, and to stuff its belly and stomach with a sort of stuffing I'd mixed with his own liver and some pig, and bread-crumbs and a kind of truffle we find near our barn by an oak, and then a little of the preserved turkey we make for the winter. And I cooked the whole beastie, with his bulging belly sewn up, in a sauce full of good red wine and good cream. Should have seen the helpings afterwards! 'Twasn't bad. Might've pleased Your Honour. It put a well-being in the whole banquet!'

Needless to say that Adèle Pidou was immediately taken on to the staff of Dodin-Bouffant on terms which she fixed herself, and that, thanks to the magistrate's deplorable weakness, she became the mistress of the house without striking a blow. Dodin, from then on, lived, according to the season, in an uninterrupted dream of veal-birds with scented stuffings, unbelievable legs of mutton under the raised skin of which lurked prodigious forcemeat balls, fricassees which made him want to live for ever, sheeps' tongues 'in curl papers' (*en papillotes*), Gascon beef-skirts, Fonbonne soups, fish broths, ducks *à la Nivernaise*, '*grenadins*' of chicken, jugged goose-livers, game sausages, stewed cockscombs, chickens *à la Favorite*, shoulders of lamb *à la Dauphine*. From savoury sausages of sucking-pig trotters in milk he went on to patties of perch and baby-quail tarts; from pâtés of plover fillets to trout in Chartreuse. No sooner was the period of baby rabbits *à la Zephyr* and baby chicks *à la follette* over, than he saw appear upon his blessed table truffles *à la Maréchale*, shrimps on the spit, partridges in their own juice, 'minute' quails, larks *au gratin*, moulds of pheasant, Polish hare, thrushes *à la Gendarme*; and later jellied boar, snipe *à la poulette*, and sandpipers *au Pontife*. Not to mention eggs *à la mouillette*, *à la bonne amie*, or *à la vestale*, omelets with anchovies *à la servante*, or *au joli coeur*, nor roe tarts, nor eels *à la Choisi*, pike *à la Mariée*, carp in Frock Coats, artichokes in Champagne wine, cardoons St Cloud, noodles with bacon, steamed mushrooms, 'tobacco-pouch' spinach, nor desserts, marchpanes, compotes, waffles and biscuits.

In this abundance of delights, surrounded by the charm of these touching meals of which each one was a new joy and none of which, unless he requested it be prepared in the same way, included a dish which had already figured upon his table, Dodin lived days of sweet satisfaction. His life, disrupted by the death of his faithful assistant, had gloriously regained its balance;

from beyond the grave Eugénie Chatagne had handed Adèle Pidou the torch of the great tradition. Perhaps, and Dodin often thought about these mysteries of fate, perhaps it was her free spirit which had led to the august and triumphal kitchen where she had officiated for so long, the woman worthy to succeed her. Having succeeded in reaching the peaks of human perfection in his art, having obtained for himself the unvarying marvels of his 'daily bread', the old magistrate, ever preaching the work of taste, suspected that his twilight would be the radiant conclusion of a beautiful life. From then on he awaited death which he did not desire but did not fear in that joyous and peaceful repletion which so many tormented and incomplete artists have never known; sure of ending his long and laborious career in the fulfilment of fruitful effort, of complete achievement, and in the ever-renewed enjoyment of each meal. Dodin finally knew all the moral and material satisfactions which cookery will yield in return for the honours due to it.

And yet, a terrible storm threatened his happiness; so true is it that our earthly condition is essentially unstable, that no man may be proclaimed happy before his death, so it is also true that the pride of princes often leads them to scorn the elementary laws of human morality and decent shame! The Prince of Eurasia dared to envy Dodin-Bouffant, his host, and coveted Adèle Pidou, the fine craftswoman of the meal which he now saw in an entirely new light. At first, his private secretary was seen roaming the market, asking questions. The next day, he took a hired cabriolet, left the city gates, and then, abandoning the vehicle in front of the salt stores, stepped with some hesitation towards the Parcels Office where Adèle went almost daily to collect some delivery of victuals. Another day, again, he was seen patiently mounting guard before the shop where Foujoullaz sold delicate early vegetables; at last, he was seen after nightfall in a suspicious waiting attitude outside the Tax Collector's gate—a house in which Adèle, her day's work done, was not too proud to visit the old cook in the quiet hours of the evening. These mysterious advances continued for some time before Dodin knew more about them than vague, imprecise rumours, subtle, uncertain noises, whispers without any consistency. This did not prevent his being most anxious about them. As an old magistrate, accustomed to sounding the depths of human hearts, to assembling circumstances in order to discover their real meaning, he half-saw, without daring to reach it, the fatal conclusion that could be drawn from the obstinate presence of the Prince's henchman in places where he was certain to meet Adèle. He had been brought up in a century, moreover, which left in the hearts of the best of Frenchmen only the frailest illusions about the gratitude of the world's Great. Dodin began to fear that he had triumphed too completely over the Heir to Eurasia. He did not quite dare confide his anxiety to Adèle, nor tell her of his fears. She was, as all true artists are, of a varying and awkward disposition, of doubtful and touchy humour, and easily irritated. He feared the possibility of a violent scene with her and a scandal which might, under the impetus of irresistible rage, deprive him of her genius. And then, was there not also at the very back of his mind a remnant of pride which forbade him to show too clearly how indispensable she had become to his existence? Could he let her know that she was the absolute sovereign of his life?

Dodin therefore carried around an anxious and tormented soul. Sometimes his imagination invented some eventuality which reason, alas, when it resumed possession of his brain, did not prove to him to be impossible. And this doubt condensed within himself, kept secret, and which he dared confide to no one, so afraid was he of formulating it in precise words, devoured him and sometimes sank him into a truly painful condition of over-excitement.

He would go out panting, bent with sorrow, mopping his brow, to flee—to go and drown his anguish in the infamous vermouths of the Café de Saxe. Noon struck. He would return, head low and despair in his heart. He would sit down and suddenly the blankness of the table-cloth would be illuminated by fillets of farm chicken *à la Pompadour*, or a mushroom stew in Chambertin, or quail *à la Mayence*, or pigeons *à la Martine* which dispersed his sorrow in a moment, as the soft breeze of a summer night scatters the last bitter smoke of burning weeds in the meadows. And the spiritual love he had conceived for the unconscious genius of the woman would seep into him, overwhelm and disarm him. He would apologize to her mentally for having doubted her; he even managed, as he consumed her absolute and perfect cooking, devoid of all weakness, free of any fault, to adorn her massive body with touching illusions, her vulgar face with beauty, and to throw her furtive glances of tenderness.

Dodin-Bouffant was too familiar with the human soul and too sceptical regarding its virtues even to dream of storming at the methods of the Highness who, having been received at his table, could consider thieving from him the happiness of his old age. This ingratitude was but a princely game. Only now and again did he take himself to task for his foolishness in setting ajar the door of his sanctuary for the royal visitor: all his thoughts and all his sufferings were really concentrated upon Adèle's possible departure—Adèle, conquered by golden promises, won over by the solicitations of her vanity; a notice which he awaited with the shudder of the 'little death' between his shoulder blades every time Adèle opened the door, every time he went home, every time he opened his eyes to those calm and pure Jurassic dawns whose tender rosiness accompanied his grilled bacon or his egg *salmis*. His life, under the shadow of this perpetual threat, became a torture that the most skilful inquisitor could not have invented, a torture complicated by his joint desire and fear to speak to the great artist from whose hands he accepted so much suffering and so much joy. This hesitation, to which every hour brought him a contradictory solution, sometimes ended by a furtive trip into town whence he would bring back some soft, silken material, some precious umbrella or chiselled brooch, humble presents which he knew quite well could never compete with the princely fortunes which could not fail to be offered to Adèle Pidou on the day when the secretary finally launched his offensive.

Had he not already launched it? Adèle, there was no possible doubt about it, was preoccupied, nowadays, sometimes dreamy. It even seemed that her natural simplicity was taking on a tinge of unaccustomed pride. She seemed to be turning over in her round head a grave problem which Dodin guessed to be the enigma of her future which she sought to solve. Her eyes often strayed far over the walls of her kitchen, and the unhappy epicure, following their direction, could see in the distance the flamboyant splendours of a palace.

He took good care, out of regard for his dignity, to mention none of his awful bitterness to his companions. But they had no trouble in detecting upon his tired and ageing features the ravages of his distress. They dared not question him, but having dimly guessed that his cook was not uninvolved in the trouble, they feared a catastrophe which lay in wait for them too.

Dodin was warned by the owner of the Café de Saxe that his apprehensions were only too well-founded. It was a terrible piece of news, for, hoping against hope, he still wished to think of his fears as chimerical. At sunset, the innkeeper had seen the cordon bleu crossing the square at the side of the elegant secretary who was speaking feverishly. She did not answer, but nodded her head. Dodin received the blow with dignity and paid for his almond-essence and kirsch, impatient to be alone. He pulled himself together with a great effort, feeling, to his surprise, almost relief at no longer struggling with uncertainty. He took an immediate decision. Rather than wait for his life to be shattered, he resolved to make the horrible sacrifice himself. Since his purse was too modest to vie with that of one of the richest princes in Europe, since Adèle had sacrificed, or was about to sacrifice, glory to vainglory and art to gold, he would himself, without awaiting her good pleasure, give her notice. In this way he would embark with dignity and of his own free will upon the obscure renunciation of his work and of his passion until Death should end it all. He pushed the door open resolutely.

Alas, prickly and frowning, for the knowledge of the crime she was about to commit soured her extremely, Adèle successively deposited before her victim roe fritters such as the Gods alone may enjoy and a calf's head in aspic *à la Vieux Lyon* which cast the master's palate, so extremely sensitive and practised, into a profound state of rapture. He threw the faithless one a loving glance and felt that he was properly lost. For, from the bottom of his heart, there rose impetuously a sentiment in which mingled, in fearsome chaos, admiration, gratitude, and, for so many indescribable joys, love. The inconstant creature would leave behind her only disaster and ruin, an empty house, a passion in ashes, a wounded heart. What a vision of oblivion passed before the eyes of that pathetic man! To be alone under this deserted roof! And, to fill the interminable hours of abandonment, to have only the disastrous prospect of vulgar and unappetizing messes! The unfortunate Dodin, urged on by who knows what, probably in the unconscious hope of seducing the woman who already had one foot on the deck of the vessel which was to bear her off for ever, began to pay her a timid and touching court which was, however, greeted with hauteur. Quite incapable himself of renouncing the heavens to which three times daily she opened the portals, he was seized with tremors of apprehension at the horrible idea that the day was nigh when her decision would be peremptorily put before him, and he had no other anxiety, day by day, than that of delaying the evil moment. Adèle, who was in all honesty of a strait-laced disposition and perhaps somewhat surprised to see her virtue attacked at this late date, sometimes deigned an absent-minded response to a fervour devoid of all salaciousness, but quickly resumed her enigmatic air, too evident a proof of her lack of conviction.

The crisis was imminent. All the premonitory signals announced it. It exploded on the first evening of winter. Dodin, like a sick man who knows himself to be condemned, was devouring in almost ferocious haste what might well be the last delights Adèle Pidou would bestow upon him. He had invited Beaubois, Trifouille, Rabaz and Magot to a dinner which he alone among them knew to be the last.

That night Adèle, after a soup of Spanish cardoon sippets, had presented a superb stuffed eel, surrounded by crystal. It had occurred to her to mix the meat of this creature, pounding it in a mortar, adding cream, breadcrumbs, chives and mushrooms, with truffles. She had wrapped this concoction around the spine of the fish, reconstituting its original shape, and covering it copiously with egg and breadcrumbs, had served it after giving it a fine colour in the oven.

Everyone had already been dazzled. The guests had then seriously tackled the hot *pâté à la Royale*, exclaiming devoutly as they seized a large piece of mutton or a fillet of partridge, or a mouthful of beef which they scooped up with generous gestures from a woodcock gravy and a rich bacon garnish which had absorbed into its thick fat the divine aroma of a clove of garlic.

Adèle, reluctant to give her master the sad news in the emotional atmosphere of a tête-à-tête, in which she would have been alone to confront a despair which she foresaw; considering moreover that the other four gourmets, as priests of the great art and habitual disciples of the Teacher, were entitled to be informed at the same time as Dodin himself; relying also somewhat upon the presence of his friends to cushion a blow she knew would be heavy; Adèle, then, had decided to announce her departure during this meal. She began just as she had laid upon the table a leg of young boar in pastry whose meat she had cushioned against the dough with a delicate hash of duck-livers marinated in champagne liqueur.

She was obviously embarrassed.

'I have to tell these gentlemen. . . .'

She did not know what to do with her hands.

'That Monsieur His Highness the Prince. . . .'

At the first words Dodin, white, taut, frozen, understood.

'He'd like to take me on . . . because he says, says he, that none of his cooks . . . well, because he was very pleased with the luncheon. . . .'

Dodin managed to sketch a bitter smile.

'I didn't want to leave M. Dodin-Bouffant . . . because . . . because it's an honour to serve a master like him . . . such a

86

connoisseur . . . so refined . . . and so good too . . . I must
tell Monsieur. . . . And then, I know all right that I've
learned a lot from Monsieur . . . he's taught me a lot . . . so
it's ungrateful. . . .'

Beaubois, Rabaz and Magot, Trifouille, understood in turn
and their faces, so recently expansive with contentment, suddenly
took on that air of painful disappointment characteristic of
children trying in vain to contain their tears.

Adèle, who must have spent much time meditating her
awkward speech, continued:

'But there it is. . . . I'm not as young as I used to be . . .
got to think of my old age. . . . And when Monsieur has gone,
what will become of me?'

This allusion to his death moved neither Dodin nor his friends
in the least.

'And I'm not rich, you know. . . . So my family advised
me . . . to accept the awfully big salary I'm being offered. . . .
His Excellency the Prince. . . . Imagine . . . sixty *écus* every
month . . . and of course an interest on the cook's perks . . .
could retire to our farm and be pretty well off. . . .'

Impelled by a sudden resolution, Dodin rose abruptly, so
unexpectedly that Adèle, terrified, thought he was going to
strike her, and his friends believed him to be in the grip of
violent madness. Very pale, very calm, on the contrary, he took
the cook by the hand and very quietly said to her:

'Adèle, I wish to speak to you.'

They both disappeared into the kitchen. A heavy silence
descended upon the table, a silence which Magot disturbed only
to observe after a few minutes of anguished thought, that the
situation would be in no way improved by the loss of the venison
if allowed to grow cold. And they began to eat sadly, occasionally

allowing to fall from their lips some emotional words about Dodin's misfortune and their own. Then, each in turn, they went back to the dish.

A long half-hour elapsed to the monotonous accompaniment of anxious chewing. At last the kitchen door opened, not without a certain majestic slowness. Dodin, now red in the face, his gaze aflame with a strange triumph and upon his features a sovereign relief, appeared holding a tearful Adèle Pidou by the hand, and spoke these simple words:

'Gentlemen: Madame Dodin-Bouffant.'

6

Pauline d'Aizery or The Fairy of the Kitchen

───◉❀◈❀│❀│◉❀◉❀◉───

What was the stuff of Dodin's conjugal fidelity? Neither his youth nor his maturity had been chaste, but his amorous adventures had always borne the stamp of a methodical, thoughtful and discreet mind, proving that his rather drab escapades sprang, not from the passionate fire of vehement adolescence but simply of an innate, sensible and well-established liking for women. The 'woman's man', later to become the happy bachelor, is not he who, at twenty, conspicuously displays a few fashionable actresses. He is the one who, quietly and privately, adds to the casual pleasures which he never disdains, those of the ten months with the little milliner, the six weeks with the young school-teacher, the glovemaker's year and the lady's maid's two seasons. Dodin-Bouffant belonged to this latter category. Throughout his life stretched an uninterrupted chain of *amours* of which he had never boasted. Had his senses not been powerful and demanding, he could never have been the great gourmet he was. In such a vigorous and definite character as his, everything marches together. However, if he had often frequented the boudoir, domain of fresh attractive soubrettes, he neglected the pantry unless he expected to find there young, beautiful and flighty cooks, which is to say hardly ever, for when they were young enough to attract him he distrusted their professional talents, despised them in other men's kitchens, and did not employ them in his own.

The reader will remember that when Eugénie Chatagne died he resisted temptation in the person of a ravishing but inefficient kitchen-maid.

Now when he married Adèle Pidou in the circumstances which we have related, he took to wife a woman of forty-six summers, short in height but of generous proportions, of a somewhat vulgar turn of countenance, without grace or charm, in which only the eyes revealed a native genius. And yet it is a fact which must be recognized that he had remained scrupulously faithful to her. His tastes, in feminine matters, did not seem to have developed so prodigiously as his gustatory senses; the springtime of his old age had accommodated itself to the vulgar and mediocre austerity of matrimony, thus contradicting the entire love-line of his life. Everywhere, save at table, he may well have been a little tired. He may, too, possibly have settled for a smooth passage towards the end of a beautiful existence without wishing to encumber its conclusion with incidents and complications. Perhaps, finally (he *could* have felt so), he may have revered within the unattractive body of Adèle Pidou, the exceptional genius which, in one soaring flight, had swept the Prince of Eurasia himself to a paradise from which exile left him inconsolable; a genius which reigned in all its infinitely varied magnificence over his own life. The Master's austere faithfulness embraced shades of all these feelings, but also certain regrets.

These latter could be divined upon seeing him stop short when the rhythm of some young and elegant walker caressed his path—the golden warmth under a picture-hat, the supple sway of disturbing forms stung his eyes with an old familiar desire. For a long time he would follow the departing apparition, mingling it in his vision with some imaginary possession, and then resume his walk in temporary melancholy.

One morning in May something occurred to move him greatly. At his desk on the ground floor, chewing a penholder and seeking an elusive rhyme, he was engaged upon the composition of a love-song for an engagement-party to which he was invited.

> *Wiles and smiles, my charming Kitty,*
> *Cannot shelter you from love. . . .*
> *The risks of being young and pretty. . . .*

Neither the words 'above' nor 'dove' would fit the last line which hovered in his mind. One side of an open window barred his view of the street from the armchair where he sat. A powdery light filled the austere study, sprinkling the dull gold bindings of his books with a festive brilliance. The slow white dust of old provincial streets floated in, wafted by the discreet breeze from nearby mountains, mingled with the scent of gardens. The reborn youth of the spring-stirred town together with the flavour of his memories disturbed his old heart and often, scorning reluctant inspiration, he would lean his head against the chair-back, close his eyes, and depart for the vanished mornings of his youthful conquests.

Suddenly a stone, a large stone, flew from the street into the room, striking a handsome piece of copper-work upon the table.

Dodin-Bouffant rose and walked to the window, prepared to upbraid the young scamps who dared to disturb his communion with the past by the effrontery of their games. The street was deserted. No doubt, after striking, the sacrilegious infants had fled around the corner into the Boulevard des Orfèvres. . . . But his gaze was drawn to a sealed letter which had been placed upon the window-sill.

He sniffed the bluish paper which gave off a strange, pleasant scent of dried herbs, examined the writing, and then greatly intrigued, had recourse to the only means of elucidating the mystery, that is to say to opening the letter. Before doing so, however, being prudent and guessing that no ordinary innocent missive would be delivered by such odd and roundabout methods, he turned the key in the lock.

'Master,

Some weeks ago you graced the table of some good friends. I was there. Dazzled by your brilliance, I heard genius speak in your voice. You awakened within me a new and unsuspected faith. My soul which had sought awkwardly to express itself in the harmonies of other arts discovered in your speech a new and incredible beauty which is the means of creation for which I languished. Since then, Master, my life has taken a new direction. I have sung the poems whose rhythms you taught me with their glowing colours, their radiance. I have understood that one can pour out one's heart in the infinite *nuances* of a long-pondered, fervently executed dish—one that can encompass happiness and melancholy, enthusiasm and weariness. Set free at last by the inspiration you have given me, I dream only of rendering you homage. Please consent to dine with me on Tuesday of next week. Freed myself by early widowhood, I respect the scruples which your own situation must necessarily suggest to you: we shall be alone in my house and at my table. No one shall know of your presence there. My staff will be dismissed for the day, and your humble servant will have the joy of serving you with her own hands . . . I live just across the frontier. Have yourself driven by mail-coach as far as Dardagny, where my country carriage which I shall be driving will await you upon the road to Vernier. I devotedly kiss the hands of my Master.

HIS PRIESTESS.'

Dodin folded the elegant sheet of paper very small and slipped it into his waistcoat pocket, unable to tear it up as prudence suggested he should. Twenty years younger, he marched up and down the study. The old magistrate, experienced in the shrewd probing of documents, read between these lines an avowal of emotions other than that of pure artistic reverence, which in itself would anyway have given him profound inner satisfaction. He breathed in happiness in great gulps, delicately balanced between the pleasure of human vanity and the joy of a possible adventure of which it sufficed him to know that he could, if he wished, taste its ultimate delights. For the philosopher, avidly peace-loving, terrified at the prospect of possible complications, had decided unhesitatingly upon reading the letter not to run the risks of the illicit love-affair which he believed to be offered him. He therefore granted himself the safe indulgence of pretending, of dreaming that he responded to the call and that he would perhaps enjoy, upon the threshold of old age, those worldly and delicate caresses, beautiful painted fruits, that his

vigorous youth had always desired and never found. He would
certainly not go to Dardagny, but he could still see himself dis-
mounting at the entrance to the little village, advancing along
the road to Vernier, and finding, by a meadow, behind a wall,
a blonde vision upon whose lips would be both the passion of a
newly-awakened vocation and the offer of an ardent tenderness.
. . . At certain moments, his soul freed itself from the contemplation of material delights and gave itself up entirely to the
pride of having perhaps inspired a really great career. . . .
From the horizon, beyond the mist-blue hills, through the open
window came an imaginary enchantment, a creamy, nutmeg
odour, the scent of a marvellous roast. . . .

Far more real was the succulent aroma which greeted him in
the passage when he emerged from the study. Adèle was in the
kitchen, preparing a dish of spring-chickens enhanced by the
last black morels of the season. And his heart, that poor heart
swayed by all the vicissitudes of appetite, melted immediately,
already oblivious of the imagined fairy-tales in grateful joy and
tender anticipation.

He spent glad, gay days then, holding himself upright, his
smile broader, his attitude more lively and alert; charmed and
rejuvenated by the fond secret he carried in his waistcoat
pocket. It seemed to him that the fair unknown had caught him
by the coat-tails to pull him back from the brink of dark old age
into bright, full sunlight. He now used a tone of protective
commiseration when talking to his companions, his 'poor'
friends who could not share the sweetness of this dear, mysterious
adventure.

But who was she, this enigmatic correspondent who had thus
suddenly rekindled the ashes of his life? He had wondered from
the moment of reading the letter, and had since asked himself the

question a thousand times. Neither a mental muster of acquaintances in the Geneva countryside, nor the recollection of young women he had met at friends' homes at Le Bugey could enlighten him. On the Tuesday, he went off as far as the Inn of the Peasant Soldier whence the mail-coach left for Switzerland. He hoped vaguely, in spite of the thing's unlikelihood, to find a clue to the identity of his unknown disciple. Even as he approached the staging-post, he duped himself deliciously; determined as he was not to leave his peaceful home to play Romeo, he saw himself climbing into the heavy vehicle, covering the miles, and then enjoying at the hands of an amorous pupil the superior pleasures offered by a young body and the inspiration of a fresh genius. He even hoped for some unexpected event to alter his decision and force his timid defences.

The coach gone, and himself quite certain that he could no longer be in time at the meeting place, his secret joy dropped from him. He felt that something had ended and that after a long-awaited and wonderful party he was about to resume the humdrum monotony of daily life.

After the Tuesday when nothing had happened, he spent the next few days in a somewhat sombre state of mind.

But suddenly at the beginning of the following week, he was again plunged into turmoil: no sooner had he sat down at his desk than a letter, this time thrown through the open casement like a boomerang, fell before him. His heart beat so violently that he had to wait a full minute before stooping to pick it up.

'I knew she would write again,' he murmured, although he had never dreamed of such a thing.

The letter, which he opened with trembling fingers, only contained three lines, which disappointed him at first sight, before he had read them.

'Master,

On Tuesday I waited, my heart full of anguish, for the arrival of the coach. Alone upon the sofa which I had arranged for you, I partook sadly of the dishes so lovingly planned for you. Next Tuesday, as last, I shall wait for you.'

Dodin's prudence wavered. The fear of complications in his life, the terror, should she discover his secret, of losing the jealous Adèle, the boredom of five hours in a stage-coach on a hot and dusty road, all these obstacles melted like soil in a swollen torrent, dwindled before the persevering call of the Fairy of the kitchen—so passionate, so mysterious. . . . At the very moment when, vanquished, he was about to take the fatal decision, he snatched at and clung by the tip of his over-excited soul, to the fact that the rendezvous was again for Tuesday, that Tuesday was the next day, and that it was really impossible for him to prepare this voyage, to accustom himself to the notion of the prospective adventure, and to explain to Adèle the reasons for absenting himself at such short notice. He heaved a sigh of which he did not know himself whether it expressed regret at making a break which would probably be a lasting one, or satisfaction at having found a plausible pretext for his renewed weakness and his reluctance to set out. But at the hour when he should have been driving towards happiness, he was tormented by bitter thoughts. There was no longer any doubt about it: he had allowed his last chance to slip through his fingers. What possibility was there, indeed, that this woman, gratuitously wounded, should continue to insist upon delighting him in spite of himself? To renew her invitation a third time she must be entirely without dignity. . . . Or, he added mentally, hardly daring to frame the thought in words, possessed by a love that dominates modesty or pride. But feeling that the Unknown would not again expose herself to the humiliation of his absence, he vowed mentally to accept the next time.

Powerless as he was to identify her, in spite of great efforts of memory and prodigious reconstruction of circumstances, sometimes he imagined her as tall, blonde and supple, at other times of medium height, dark and well-rounded. To be sure, his powers, unaffected by the years, still required no stimulus; but whenever he pictured his Unknown within his arms, Madame Dodin-Bouffant could not guess to what fantastic romancing she owed the renewal of favours to which her husband's age and habits had long since unaccustomed her. Of course, it is also true that Dodin very often pleased himself by clothing the Unknown in the pure form of the Muse Gastera, tendering to his nostrils the incense of a glorious cuisine.

At bottom, the *gastronome* felt strangely ashamed of his husbandly virtue. Still imbued with the spirit of a century when scruples of this sort were not common currency, he would conclude that his constancy was petty, vulgar, and foolishly naïve. How his friends and companions would mock if they knew he was faithful! What half-pitying laughter would greet the revelation that Dodin-Bouffant, the Great Dodin-Bouffant, poet of epicureanism, master of divine sensuality, had refused at the same time the offer of a girl and a banquet! Had he not then forfeited the final gift of Fortune? Had not Life, which had been good to him, wished him to enter old age with the fond memory of this last love he had failed to seize? Had it not, to beautify his imminent decrepitude, raised this supreme autumn fruit, a beautiful, healthy, rose-gold apple offered to him at twilight as Eve offered it to Man at the world's dawn?

On Friday, at eleven in the morning, as he was the first to

arrive at the daily rendezvous at the Café de Saxe, Mme Hermine, the landlord's wife, handed him a letter which a carter had left upon the counter and which was addressed to him. Glancing at the envelope, Dodin in one second turned green, white, red, all the colours of the syrups and liqueurs around the counter. He had recognized 'the' writing.

He was alone. Trifouille and Beaubois had not yet arrived; Rabaz and Magot were slowly crossing the square, stopping at each step the better to buttonhole each other in discussion. Dodin-Bouffant had time to glance at the letter. He read it, half-hiding it beneath the table.

'Master,

Tuesday I shall *still* wait for you. . . . I have set two duck-lings to marinate in an ancestral marc for a stuffed duckling tart; and I am considering a dish of eels *à la poulette*. There will be roses everywhere and I shall wear a flowered organdie for you.'

Dodin crammed the letter into his pocket. His two friends came in and Rabaz and Magot did not fail to notice his absent-mindedness during the customary apéritif. He took hardly any part in the conversation, save to angle it occasionally upon subjects close to that which occupied his heart. He was lost in a dream, and did not even pay attention to the Island Wine which drew from him daily exclamations of admiration. Only when Trifouille ridiculed certain senile passions for young girls, and Rabaz congratulated old age upon being the happy time when one is at last freed of the cares of the flesh, did Dodin take fire and defend an instance which he alone knew, by placing it in a general theory of the beauty, experience and earnestness which only an elderly man can bring to love.

The conversation proceeded, somewhat untidily, and little

by little his resolution took shape. The better to let it unfold, he felt the need for solitude, and went off on a pretext which rather surprised his friends, towards the staging-post. He walked slowly, in the shadow of the double row of limes, hat in hand and misty-eyed. In fact, since he had had time to reflect, such a tumult of thoughts bumped about in his brain that, despairing of sorting them out, and abandoning any attempt to co-ordinate them, he yielded himself up to their confusion. A single light shone upon this ocean-like fog which he no longer tried to pierce: this time, he would go. . . . He felt it, he knew it, he wished it. Why was he so determined after having put up such a determined resistance? Because the metal of duty cannot long defy the flaming breath of passion; because the vehement love which betrayed itself in the insistence of the Unknown sang like a siren around his pride; because words have a magic virtue and because the tender missives had slowly awakened in his depths a youthfulness of heart which he had not suspected; because a tiny tremor, light as the breezes that dimple the surface of a stream, a tiny tremor had passed through his soul; because a duckling tart and eels *à la poulette* are temptations irresistible to a palate capable of imagining their flavours beforehand; because, in short, he had conceived at the time when he was refusing the invitations, a purely speculative plan which would remove from his escapade any danger of conjugal suspicion. Yes, his wife. . . . He thought suddenly that he must tell her of this voyage, reminding himself of the excellent reasons he would advance in explanation. But the Master, being a good man, was a poor liar, and he was longing to get his mendacious discourse over. Moreover, it was nearly lunchtime, and he was counting upon a trout pâté. He therefore hastily turned his steps homewards.

As he savoured that pâté, he nearly abandoned his criminal

99

designs. Adèle had prepared it herself, and its perfection brought tears to the epicure's eyes. How had the truffled larding mingled with the anchovies and melted partly into the rosy flesh of the fish? How had the blonde pie-crust imbibed its juices and given them its own smoothness? All Adèle's magical art was needed to accomplish such a miracle! Deceive such an artist? Betray this superior being who daily dispensed so much happiness?

Dodin nearly gave up his plan. But he found that the chicken-forcemeat balls which followed this handsome entrée, though they would have plunged a lesser gourmet than himself into ecstasies, were not quite the thing. They had initially been subjected to an over-lively flame, and then the gravy was a trifle too thin. Dodin was brought back to a more perfidious and perhaps a more balanced view of things.

A Septmoncel, a cheese which he adored, whose earthy pallor was exactly as it should be, marbled with green veinings, was brought in, and he announced casually:

'On Tuesday I shall take the nine o'clock coach for Geneva. . . . Next Tuesday. I am a trifle worried about certain Swiss mining shares. . . .'

The argument was irresistible to Adèle, who owed to her peasant origins a very precise sense of money values. And because Dodin had also to explain why this journey with a purely financial purpose involved his wearing gala clothes, he added:

'My banker, moreover, has invited me to a meal. Oh! I'm not too delighted with that. . . . I don't care for parties with these Genevese gentlemen who feel they are doing you a favour by condescending. . . .'

Dardagny appears over the rise; a little puddle of dark roofs in the green plain, in the centre of a motionless army of vines as

100

yet showing little more than their stakes. Already Dodin-Bouffant can see, among the cloud-like tops of tall trees, the castle which he knows well, the double-pillared portico, the handsome wrought-iron balcony, and the clumsy towers. His gaze wanders, somewhat vaguely, from the hillock of Challex to the peak of Oz, takes in the Vuache and the Mont de Sion, and returns obstinately to the ravine along the road to St Jean de Gonville. It is not upon this road that She will be waiting, but as it is the only road he can see at the moment, his hopefulness clings to it desperately. His heart beats furiously. Mentally he chides himself, simultaneously ashamed and delighted to find himself at his age as moved as Cherubino. As a provincial of the longest standing he has taken this road innumerable times, the road one cannot avoid taking to leave the town in a north-easterly direction. For the first time he does not appraise the quality of the swift London river trout, nor the condition of the vineyard across the stream, climbing the rise from Peicy to Russin. *Who* is she who waits for him at the end of the road? How will she appear to him? Fate will have indulged him to the last, enveloping his final and most beautiful adventure in mysterious emotions. His long experience, his refinement, rejoice in the protraction of the story which has allowed him for some time now to imagine the charms of the unknown beckoner, so that reality may not disappoint the dream. So he tries to stifle in philosophy a discomfort which increases with every wheel-turn. He is soon forced to admit that his beating heart is not alone responsible—so moved is he that a definite anguish grips his entrails.

Dardagny! Already! With some difficulty, he descends. He is not quite in this world. Where is the road to Vernier, which, however, he knows quite well? Unseeingly, he passes the little terraces of the Castle and its groves of chestnut trees. Far away the Alps spread out in a soft blue line, pierced, as if by heaven-aimed pick-strokes, by the muffled ghosts of the Dents d'Oche. It is a long village; he crosses it pantingly, envious of the un-worried *vignerons* drinking outside the inns with no suspicion of Pleasure's inviting torment. At last, he finds his way. At the last house, he turns left: the road, and yet it *is* the road to Vernier, is empty, with that brilliant and dusty emptiness of nearby summer.

He stops and sighs with relief. No one. What a blessing! He came. He acted as a man; but the adventure is now over, since she is not at her rendezvous. Through his mind flashes the suspicion of a practical joke—the jokers will be no better off, they will have succeeded only in giving him a delicious outing. He will catch the Jura coach which passes again at eleven, and that will give him time to arrange for Mère Niclet, at Choully, to prepare for him one of those chicken fricassees which she alone can make to perfection. And what supple, fresh, Satigny wine he will drink with it!

Promptly freed from his amorous concerns, he begins to notice the charm of the handsome rolling plain, stretching through vine and village, forest and ravine, to the Jura, up to the solemn and haughty Salève, brilliant with the moist light of the invisible Lake of Geneva.

He walks slowly now, with short steps, renewing his friend-ship with the old habit of dawdling. On his right, a clover field is an incarnadine splash of colour; the transparent, burnt, vinous colour of those wonderful Morgons. On his left, the mossy wall of a park which breaks off a few steps farther on, cut off by a narrow path which separates it from an ocean of young corn.

Just before reaching the end of the wall, Dodin stops short, nostrils flaring, eyes round, eyebrows raised, his whole face moonlike with astonishment. A hand, raised to wipe his brow, remains frozen in mid-air, and only, between the revers of his open frock-coat, his prominent abdomen flutters with a message from his heart. Behind the angle of the wall, from a mass of leafy bushes, a nose-tip, an eye and a wisp of fair hair emerge: and this half-profile scans the road. And now follows an adorable head haloed in a mass of golden curls, a young, full, proud figure whose arm, drawn back, leads a graceful horse harnessed to a pale blue stanhope. Two bright and laughing eyes, an indescribable mouth, disperse the embarrassment of the moment by mimicking to perfection the gaping roundness of Dodin's expression. A tiny hand takes his frozen one from mid-air and leads him to the carriage which has stopped beside him, and there he is, upon the narrow seat, pressed, yes truly pressed, against the most tempting body an epicure could dream of.

He had remembered the face as soon as he saw it behind the wall. Now, casting side-long glances at it, for he did not dare turn his head to face her, he recalled the setting in which they had met. He saw himself, not long ago, in a comfortable house at Bossey with his old friends, bowing to a young widow, Mme Pauline d'Aizery. To this recollection, for his was an essentially gastronomic memory, was added that of a wild-boar *daube*. . . . In excellent form that day, he had waxed lyrical about the imperious rules for cooking game, the powerful charm of its scent, its juices which have something in common with the fine wines of Burgundy. He had been at his best—he remembered having used poetic and felicitous expressions, and he had indeed noticed at the time, and forgotten immediately afterwards, that Madame Pauline d'Aizery followed his lecture with a passionate display of interest, appearing quite uplifted, her adorable eyes lighting up with a metaphysical sparkle.

The horse climbed along the slope to Russan at a walk.

Propitious bumps and lurches threw their bodies against each other without Pauline making the slightest attempt to avoid these collisions. One of them brought her hair to brush against the happy gourmet's cheek. But Dodin was very anxious. How to behave in such circumstances? Until then, the Master had conquered exclusively in a milieu where women, though their honour be equal to that of ladies of fashion, consider it pointless to struggle overmuch, only to reach a little later, but inevitably, the same eternal situation and its accompanying gestures. Had his companion been a milliner, a soubrette or a dancing-mistress, he would have put his arm around her waist, and shortly afterwards dropped a kiss in her hair, behind the ear. But, warm as her attitude was, how would Madame Pauline d'Aizery receive such a grenadier's demonstration of love? There must be a ritual for plucking the fruits of her class. Which? And on the other hand, if, as her letters allowed him to suppose, Madame d'Aizery had decided in advance upon the most precise extremes, what would she think of his reserve, and how surprised would she be at his naïvety? The honest Dodin-Bouffant, more expert in matters of the table than in those of the heart, had no idea that Pauline d'Aizery had already seen through his embarrassment, indeed, had foreseen it, and being venturesome, free and sensual, had found her sentimental admiration titillated by the prospect of a new amusement in conquering a 'great man'. Within him she sensed a greediness which, properly handled, was capable of devotion to objects other than those of the table, and of involving senses other than that of taste. To be near, to have, to hold, Dodin-Bouffant, famous throughout France, and Europe too since the witty episode of the Prince of Eurasia! This gastronomic passion was certainly more original than the Parisian cooings in the fashionable novels of tearful poets!

But a fear seized her: Dodin must remain completely, absolutely, a *gastronome*; the amorous state in which she wished to put him must not reduce him to the size of mere mortals. Had Musset been seated beside her instead of the uncontested master of cookery, she would not have tolerated his addressing her otherwise than in alexandrines.

She was soon to be reassured. Dodin-Bouffant, who had decided during a long silence to accentuate, without appearing to do so, the accidental but delicious contacts caused by the bad road, drew back suddenly, his face contorted, overcome by a sudden anguish. A thought had crossed his mind:

'Madame,' he gasped. 'In your first letter you told me you intended to send your servants away for the day—that we should be alone. . . .'

'Yes, well?'

'But who, at this precise moment, is watching your eels, fervently surveying the progress of your ducklings? Everything will burn, or at least cook too rapidly!'

A heaven-sent joyful exaltation filled her. Here was the Dodin-Bouffant she loved, having glanced into his mind. The more legendary but almost as real Dodin her imagination had painted in the colours and gilt of an idol while she waited, preparing for him the meals he never came to share.

'Set your mind at rest, great man. I have been working for you since five o'clock this morning, as I did last Tuesday, and the Tuesday before, and the person to whom I have confided the task of watching over my creations for an hour (and who will disappear as soon as she hears the horse's hooves in the courtyard), is worthy of the responsibility. We shall be alone, as I promised you, and the eels will not be fried up, nor the ducklings burnt.'

When the stanhope entered the garden of Madame d'Aizery's

villa, things were going famously. The bold sensuality of the young woman delighted in Dodin-Bouffant's timidity. She felt him to be ardent but embarrassed; the fire within him could not quite pierce the ashes of his inexperience. She tasted fully the pleasure she had promised herself in setting out to conquer her great man.

There was no name on the gate of the villa, but the lintel offered to guests and travellers these lines of Horace:

'What, then, is this great unknown which the wise call Good—sovereign and supreme Good?'

The state of mind, the moral attitude revealed by this sceptical and perhaps epicurean device did not escape the attention of Dodin who was a connoisseur of old authors. His subtlety returned to him by degrees, as he grew used to his paradoxical situation; it reassured him to realize that he would not have to attempt a task outside the limit of his own experience, and that thanks to an odd but eminently convenient whim of his blonde hostess, he need only await, whilst accepting her homage, the moment when he himself would decide to yield.

The tall wheels grated upon white gravel. From the high seat it seemed to Dodin that he was sailing upon an ocean of roses: red, yellow, white, they balanced their fleshy, scented bunches upon bouquets of tender greenery; creamy or scarlet pompoms jostled each other up painted arches; there were wild, incoherent sheaves of eglantines; roses of tender pink fell back like rosy cascades of water, purple ones flamed and white, waxen ones languished; some, ochre-coloured, seemed carved in living amber. Dodin, gently rocked by a sweet excitement, breathed in their perfume and allowed the fantasy of their many colours to thrill his faraway gaze through half-closed eyelids.

The villa was built of the greenish stone of Meillerie, in the comfortable, massive style of Genevese country houses. The interior was pleasant, with a very special feminine quality: disdainful of mere prettiness, and suggesting a concern for profound sensuality rather than the vanity of superficial impressions. All the seats invited relaxation; the colours enfolded rather than pleased the eye. The little drawing-room where Pauline installed him felt sweetly mysterious. Pale yellow, the shade of certain petals in the rose-garden, was the dominant colour of great floating draperies which masked walls, doorways and angles, blurring all the precise lines of the room. The sofas, long and broad, on which were soft, downy cushions, seemed to draw the guest into their gentle laps. Floating in two black and copper bowls, large russet leaves opened like flat eyes. And Dodin felt himself penetrated by an insinuating, fresh, peppery perfume which hung over everything. The window, overlooking the Rhone plain, opened upon sky and emptiness, framed only a narrow band of water on the left bank, beyond a chalky cliff-lip, and farther away a clump of greenery around the sails of the Ratte windmill and the roofs of Aire-la-Ville. Dodin, far, so far, away from the ancestral furniture of his old house, from its sharp outlines and polished wood, allowed himself to drift upon his dream. Adèle, Beaubois, Trifouille, the Café de Saxe . . . all that was now vague and foggy, in another country, another planet, non-existent.

'I shall leave you tête-à-tête with this, and return to the kitchen to look after your happiness,' she murmured very low, brushing his shoulder with her bosom. And she pointed at two glasses and a bottle upon an occasional table. Dodin-Bouffant, emerging with an effort from his daze, immediately recognized an excellent Portuguese wine, an Ervedosa from the vineyards of Mesdames Conceicoes whose sweet, virile flavour mingled in his mouth with the kiss Pauline had allowed him to snatch as she went.

He began to inspect the setting for the collapse of his marriage vows, for Adèle only became vaguely real to him when he noted, most hopefully, that he was probably about to deceive her. To be truthful, although the quality of the wine seemed to disprove it, the drawing-room appeared to him a far more suitable frame for love than for great gastronomy: an elegant boudoir seldom promises a serious dining-room. But, although he felt some slight remorse, he was ready to betray, at the same time as he betrayed Adèle, the art for which she stood. Let the meal but be decent—for he would not temporize, even on the most vital pretexts, and insisted upon a minimum of propriety—and he was ready to sacrifice, without the slightest reservations, this day of Aphrodite to the pleasures of the flesh.

He caressed a hand-mirror, a sweet-box, a muslin scarf, scattered upon the tables and on the back of a love-seat, enjoying these foretastes of rapture in which so many reflections and vibrations of her charm were imprisoned.

Of course, the delicious, fashionable young creature that she was could not possibly have devoted more than good intentions and no doubt a positive instinct for pleasure to the great art of gastronomy. That art exacted lengthy meditation which she could hardly enjoy, experience which she had had no time to acquire, and genius ill-assorted to frivolity. Dodin-Bouffant, taken out of himself, drunk upon illusory youth, filled with amorous hope, did not mind. He, who had been unable to accept the Crown Prince of Eurasia's banquet without showing his indignation, was now quite resigned. The exceptional charm of the circumstances had conditioned his state of mind more easily than he would have believed possible.

Pauline d'Aizery half-opened the door, and, as she had done by the road-side wall, stuck her charming little head through the opening, conferring precision upon the romantic dreams of the *gastronome*. Emboldened by the recent kiss, very gallantly, he seized his glass in his right hand as she came nearer, and attempted, without incurring her apparent displeasure, to give his charming friend small sips of wine, with his left arm around her handsome shoulders, half-bared by a summer gown.

'And now to table,' she cried gaily, 'and as we are alone I shall wait upon you myself.'

The dining-room was more solemn than he had expected; panelled in mahogany it was nobly and soberly decorated by painted or carved gastronomic attributes. Several handsome bottles upon a dresser offered the guest a shining, transparent welcome. He noticed at once that the sturdy, long and broad table was drawn up beside a large sofa upholstered in maroon cloth, its cushions of the same material being stitched and buttoned like an eiderdown—it was the only seat in the room.

An arrangement of pillows marked their two places, side by side, facing imposing cutlery, china and glasses whose size and profusion at any rate were encouraging. Upon this table steamed an enormous sausage, not very long but equally tall, swelling its crisp, transparent, juicy skin. Pauline pierced it with a fork, releasing a tiny jet of perfumed juice whose robust quality quite mastered the scent of the three roses on the distant sideboard.

Once more in earnest, for nothing, quite definitely, could prevail upon the major importance of a meal, Dodin tasted the rosy meat and felt surprised: in spite of his efforts, he could not identify any ingredient of ordinary pork-butchery. After a visible mental struggle, his face suddenly lit up with solemn happiness. He had managed to isolate the flavours of several unexpected meats, of rare herbs, of fiery spices mingled, he thought, with far-off echoes of cream and wine. He was amazed at the innovation, and put down his fork, but before he could express his admiration Pauline, who was filling one of his glasses, said:

'You will see how well the rather highly-flavoured Vaumorillon accompanies this hors d'oeuvre.'

And she sat down, not beside him but against him. He swept her with a glance so moved that he need not speak. She murmured, as if she had already given herself: 'Are you happy?'

They were so close that his only answer was to rest his head upon her shoulder. With an air of fond weariness, she bent her forehead and caressed him with her hair. Then she raised him gently.

'Master,' she said seriously, 'it is time to fetch the eels—one minute too long. . . .'

The argument was irresistible.

'Go, Pauline,' said Dodin-Bouffant, daring for the first time to use her Christian name.

It was pure enchantment. The fish, caught in a swift-flowing stream, was perfectly fat, all its beautiful white flesh impregnated with a flavour of wild herbs and limpid water, but this only served to confirm the impeccable sureness of the hostess's choice. What revealed her full genius was the sauce. Not one error marred its pure harmony. The experienced gourmet's palate tenderly discovered its delicate shadings blended into an impressive and seductive whole. Having eaten, slowly, in the silence of profound reverence, he laid down his fork and enveloped Madame d'Aizery in a look of loving emotion. This prolonged though silent admission of enthusiasm over, half-choked by the blossoming of this unexpected brilliance, he stammered:

'Pauline, Pauline. . . . How did you . . . how did you manage?'

'For you, I took a great deal of trouble. . . . And when one feels deeply about an art. . . . It is you who inspired me!'

'Yes, but not one fault—not a single one. . . . How did you achieve that impeccable range of glowing flavours?'

'I chose my ingredients slowly and with scrupulous care,' she said, sparkling with triumph. 'For instance, to make the stock, I tried more than five white wines, and finally selected a Lorraine, from Dornot, little known outside the region, but whose heady yet earthy flavour seemed designed to bathe eel flesh. My butter! what trouble I had finding it as I wished, half-fat, but from clover-fed cows! And my twenty little onions. People think they can put any breed of onions into a dish! . . .'

She had spoken feverishly, set afire once more by her inspiration, while Dodin, his mouth full, concentrated his entire attention and his sense of taste upon following and checking Pauline's explanations which raised him to a level of refinement which even he, Dodin-Bouffant, had not fully explored. He was really handsome to look upon at that moment and his air of enjoyment with dignity would have stirred even a woman who was not in love with him or with his fame. Glowing with emotion and surprise, for he was discovering masterly genius where he had hoped to find no more than a pleasing amateur talent, the noble epicureanism of his features stood out more prominently, the passion in his eyes lit up their darker depths, the sensual flare of his nostrils enhanced the firm line of his nose, the faint quiver of his lips gave them a mysterious life of their own; his cheeks, below the white whiskers, curved nobly.

Once again, Pauline looked at him tenderly, brimming with pride at having inflamed the soul of the illustrious gourmet. Eyes half-closed, pouting slightly, she advanced her lips in a childish moue, murmuring:

'Still happy?'

Dodin-Bouffant simply accepted the ardent kiss which absolved him from answering. And the sweet Anjou of a Clos des Buandières scented their mouths' long, deep caresses, rejoicing their mutual greed. They were two simultaneously inspired poets, expressing their heavenly exaltation by silent gestures only.

Events were moving rapidly. They had arrived, upon the road of love, at that point where the same final preliminaries are equally appropriate to a marquise and a chambermaid, a bourgeoise and a peasant-girl. The city is taken by a score of different strategies—the final assault is always launched in the same manner, at the double. It became obvious that the conclusion was at hand, and that, in a few moments, the great man, like all great men, would have his Egeria. But suddenly they leapt up together and exclaimed in identical tones of anguish:

'The ducklings!'

Pauline rushed to the kitchen. She was in time, but only just. Anyway, nothing was compromised. Triumphantly she brought in the beautiful golden pie. Her walk had the rhythm of supreme assurance conferred upon it by the Master's admiration—henceforward all hers—by the self-confidence that sprang from it, and by her certainty of ultimate victory.

Before allowing him to break the swelling pie-crust, she filled their glasses—so carefully, so solicitously!—with a Gevrey, Clos de la Perrière, whose smooth sap, delicacy and dazzling bouquet floated in a warm translucence of deep and tender colour. Then she heaped her guest's plate with the most astonishing pie imaginable. The scent, freed from its captivity under the pastry, filled the room, bracing, sharp and intoxicating.

Dodin-Bouffant, bewildered by the complex perfection of his happiness, took a first forkful: he had deftly taken some meat,

some pie-crust and some stuffing together. In short, he was about to absorb a synthesis. It was a kind of vertigo—he was biting into the Absolute. Euphoria rose to his brain. His palate encompassed that perfect realization whereby certain rare masterpieces fuse with the eternal and the divine.

Pauline read this enchantment upon his ecstatic features. She felt that from the peaks where she had already raised him, he had soared still further in one single flight. She herself, in the full expansion of her greed, her pride and the imminent satisfaction of her desire, leaned against her lover like a beautiful plant bowing to the tepid breezes of early spring. But his gentle hand restrained her.

'Let us not allow it to grow cold. Let us eat first and I shall tell you later. . . .'

And the pie was eaten in a silence of mingled embarrassment and respectful admiration.

As Pauline, a trifle piqued, anxious, and ill at ease, rose to change the dishes and pour the wine, Dodin, master of the solemn authoritative gesture, froze her with a raised hand.

'Madam, we have been on the brink of an abyss. I do not blush at all at the pressing homage your beauty extracted from me. Was it possible that I should remain indifferent to your splendid flesh, unmoved by your generous nature so like my own? By calling me to your side with a touching insistence for which I thank Heaven, you showed your conviction that a mutual passionate cult of the table sprang from a mutual ardour of temperament, more complete and more general, reaching beyond the bounds of greed alone; from the beginning we tacitly decided to yield to the conclusion of this logical development. In this I was encouraged by the unforeseen proof of what I called to myself your "taste", at the very first mouthful of your memorable sausage; at your masterpiece of eels, above all; my scruples, my duty, my vows which your presence alone had already so gravely compromised, finally vanished . . . certainty sprang from their ashes: I had found in you an Adèle Pidou, young, scented, well-born, elegant—the Inspiration in short that the musician, the poet, so often find upon their path, which the gourmet never encounters and which had been the hopeless dream of my whole life. You were there!'

Pauline d'Aizery, standing by the table in the attitude in which Dodin's speech had frozen her, felt her heart beat faster. The *gastronome* continued:

'But your duckling pie arrived. From the first mouthful it became emphatically clear to me that the excellence of this meal was not the result of fortune's favouring an amiable hobby, but that it was due to genius. . . . Yes, I say genius, great genius, that is to say a willed conception, of mysterious inspiration, of admirable method! And so, having met my match—nay, my superior—I have no longer the right to use you for my pleasure, nor even for yours. I must believe that you love me since, in spite of my silence, you called me to you three times. I admit it the more readily, Madam, as I myself have loved you since your first letter. Now, as a man to whom you have given a young heart again without erasing its old experience, let me say that love festers like a wound when possession does not finally lead to the plenitude of joint existence. Between us, is this possible? Am I not imprisoned in my life, in my gratitude to a helpmeet who has already given me fifteen years of devotion and not one failed meal? Am I not a prisoner of my daily round? And you yourself, out of respect for our art, would you advise me to abandon to sorrow and oblivion a good woman who has always been faithful to her own high standards, affording me the daily pleasure of her masterpieces? So? I admit it to my shame: had I encountered in you no more than an ingenious amateur of culinary pastimes, I should have yielded to the imperious demands of my desire without a thought of what I was destroying. It was my, alas infamous, intention until the eels. But the duckling pie revealed to me peremptorily that I had not the right to massacre an artist's soul like yours. What would your genius, your enthusiasm, become in the nerve-racking intervals between our rare and difficult meetings, in the impatience of a solitary existence which would seem the more empty to you for allowing me to share it occasionally, hoping in vain for impossibilities? They would dry up, dust would settle upon them, the ashes of weariness would stifle them. This noble art which touches upon every aspect of life, expresses all its shades of meaning, models itself upon all its vicissitudes, escorts and comments upon our hearts' adventures: you might succumb to the folly of no longer wishing to cultivate it save for myself, almost constantly absent, which is to say never. Also, like all great human creations, cookery, great cookery, can only be achieved in inspiring conditions of happiness which would be denied you. What sort of gastronomic works are those that reveal only an embittered and disappointed soul? No, I have no right to strangle your inspiration. This dawn of yours already shines upon magnificent destinies. My incomplete love could only bring mists to your morning brightness. I have not the right, *I have not the right*, to destroy an inspired being. What a mockery, if, having devoted my whole life to proclaiming my faith, I murdered upon its altar a new-born prophetess! With the fervour of an old man whom a young and pretty woman condescends to notice, I should have taken the love you offered me, had you not been the artist you are!'

Dodin drained his glass of Gevrey and mopped his brow. In

this speech, gushing up from his heart to his lips, he had sanctified a passionate life and buried fifty years of dreams.

As for Pauline d'Aizery, caught in a trap of her own making, she felt, in spite of herself, her humbled pride evaporating in the warmth of his great ingenuous conviction. She had wanted to become the great man's mistress and his inspiration without calculating the unforeseen consequences of proving to him, as she had wished to, the legitimacy of her ambition. She had thought to attack and carry off Dodin-Bouffant with the complicity of his exalted senses; she had not divined that sensuality, when it rises above itself, has a morality and a purity of its own. She had seen Dodin-Bouffant, the epicure, on earth, but had failed to see Dodin-Bouffant, the apostle, among the stars.

However, she was sufficiently flattered by the Master's reverence, her self-respect soothed and comforted, so that the end of the luncheon, although clouded by some restraint, remained free of apparent bitterness. In fact, Pauline quivered with a warming pride at the praises Dodin heaped upon the cardoons in cheese sauce, the custards, the cakes and the dessert wines—she had drawn cries of admiration from the illustrious man whom the Prince of Eurasia's banquet had left dissatisfied!

She accompanied her guest to await the coach, respectful, dignified, a trifle sad, but somewhat reassured by his promise to return . . . and by hope.

As the approaching vehicle raised the dust of the long village street, Dodin seized her hands. He looked at her with eyes in which regret flashed by as rapidly as a glistening trout in a stream.

'My child,' he said, 'you have given me one of the most wonderful meals of my life. But for the last hour I have been wondering: what can you possibly have prepared on the two Tuesdays when I did not come?'

7

The Crisis

———◗●◖●◗●◖●| ✻ |●◗●◖●◗●◖———

Although his greatness, which was real, was generally recognized and made of him a figure somewhat larger than life, Dodin was but a man. Thirty years of rich and excellent fare at last succeeded in undermining his still powerful physique. It was a possibility he had already envisaged long ago, and which he contemplated philosophically, with a serene soul. But when, on the morning of 6 November, he was rudely awakened by an acute pain gripping his right toe, when he saw his foot swollen, when he felt, as well as continuous deep cramps, regular and more acute attacks of an unbearable tearing nature, he was obliged to admit to himself that reality far outstripped the illness he had imagined as probable. However, foreseeing that complaints appropriate to the extent of his sufferings would expose him to the most unendurable bourgeois moralizing upon gastronomic hygiene, excesses at table, and the dangers of generous wines and elaborate dishes, he managed to put a fairly good face on it before his guests, stifling his sighs and

117

limiting the expression of his pain to a few grimaces.

He had already sent for Doctor Bourboude in the early morning, not reposing in Rabaz the same confidence as a doctor as in his gourmet's capacity.

Bourboude, naturally, had no trouble in diagnosing an attack of gout.

'And,' he added, 'this is a mild one. You will soon be rid of it. It is up to you whether you are prepared to face a second, longer and more violent. Should you prefer not to, there is only one means: diet. Convinced as I am that you will not submit to regular and strict rules of health, I leave to you, at your own risk and peril, your midday meal. But cut out meat at supper-time. It is your only remaining chance of not being caught again, and more severely.'

Dodin listened to the doctor with a serious and restrained air. The sadness of the alternative gaping before him managed momentarily to stifle the tortures of his crisis. A diet! He, Dodin-Bouffant, on a diet! His anguish contained not only all the hideous reality of that essentially anti-gastronomic word, but also a sort of shame, of humiliation, an ironical melancholy.

He could see himself in the mirror upon the mantelpiece opposite his bed. What remained, now, of the sprightly Dodin-Bouffant who had stirred Pauline d'Aizery's heart? How swiftly she would have been cured could she have seen his flesh coarsened by illness, his eyes dimmed with suffering, his sudden collapse into the very depths of his sixty-five years to the brink of which he had clung for so long! And were she to hear that he was on a diet. . . .!

However, pain imprinted upon his mind the abhorred prescription: no meat at night. These words of Bourboude's assumed within him and in spite of himself, an authority which he now denied but feebly . . . the more so as, by dint of turning them over and over in his head, he succeeded in reducing their meaning to the letter of the law, in limiting, impoverishing, rendering them almost harmless. If, in exchange for the con-cession to which his ingenious greed had reduced the doctor's prescription, he could escape the torture which had been racking him for forty-eight hours, life could, in short, through this compromise, still be bearable.

The crisis did indeed cease quite soon as Bourboude had fore-seen.

Dodin, torn between the burning memory of pain which he trembled to think of experiencing again, perhaps even more intensely, and the intuitive horror he felt for the word Diet, shut himself up with Adèle to plan the first of the severe evening meals ordained by the Faculty. That night, therefore, after lengthy discussions, he was served a thick bisque, well seasoned and full of shrimp-tails, cardoons *au gratin*, and the first truffles of the season, wrapped in bacon and paper and baked in hot wood-ash. A good piece of Septmoncel cheese and an apple pie with cream completed this 'modest' meal.

'No meat,' he kept repeating to himself, 'Bourboude would be pleased with me.'

As he was more certain of observing the letter rather than the spirit of the law, he prudently used 'would' instead of 'will', indicating clearly enough that he did not intend to submit his interpretation of the diet for the approval of the man of science. . . .

And Dodin, with a supreme cowardice which he tried at first to disguise from himself, but to which he quickly became accustomed, settled down into his mendacity and organized it skilfully.

'Meat is not flesh,' he explained to Adèle, 'and light, easily digested fish is not forbidden to me. I shall not, of course, over-indulge in it. . . .'

From then on Dodin's diet gravitated between garlic mayonnaise and stuffed artichoke bottoms, smooth triple-broths with dumplings and incomparable onion fricassees, cardoons in every shape and form, various mushrooms with every kind of garnish, abundant truffles and cheese *gratins*, thick *fondues* and roe tarts. Richly dressed celery and endive, shrimp sauces, Provençal snails, plovers' eggs *à la Dubarry*, tarts and ramekins, omelets with asparagus tips or tunny-fish, eggs *à la Bressane*, with anchovies, or Bearnaise sauce, bacon macaroni, or *à la Demidoff*, or again with Madeira sauce, potatoes in pastry, potato cakes, potatoes creamed or *à la Barigoule*, risottos, Lorraine salads, Impératrice, Lucifer and Prince of Wales salads, cucumbers *à la poulette*, fried glazed spinach, aubergines *à la Palikare*—all these graced Dodin's board from seven o'clock onwards, where there also flowed oceans of Bordelaise and Gaillarde, Grand Veneur and Indienne, Mirepoix and Rouennaise, Sainte Ménéhould and Sultana sauces.

From time to time, about twice a week, the Master, winking like a schoolboy planning an escapade, would murmur to Adèle: 'Let's be a little wild, just for once. . . .' And that night the Saint Marceau or Flemish soup, the cress or parmesan cream would be replaced by a spitted eel, a *gibelotte* of fish, a pike in Périgord fashion, or a pâté of trout.

And when his palate discovered any traces of meat in a stuffing or a sauce, he took good care not to inquire about it, affecting to abandon himself without anxiety to the strictness of Adèle and her assistant who, as the memory of the crisis faded, multiplied these breaches of the rules in the ever stronger belief that the doctor's diet, if adhered to, would debilitate the Master!

He, since eliminating meat from his evening meals, had acquired the habit of taking certain serious precautions during the day. At four o'clock, with a strong cup of milky coffee, he would have some marzipan tartlets, or a cherry muscadine, or an apple charlotte, or pineapple cakes, Toulouse puff pastries, various puddings, tea-flavoured custard or a pistachio soufflé—sometimes simply a dozen stuffed pancakes, the whole always accompanied by fresh waffles, marchpanes and brioches.

Sometimes he would have his afternoon tea at the Café de Saxe where he had ordered some specialty a day before : Calville apples in violet jelly, which they made perfectly, a chocolate cake, a pear stew *à la Cardinale*, an apple mousse or an omelet *à la Celestine*. On these occasions, unable to drink the coffee served in that establishment, he would have his own brought over from the house to be kept warm in the bain-marie; alternatively, he drank their Island wine which he esteemed so highly.

Dodin-Bouffant sometimes met Doctor Bourboude, without the slightest pleasure. When in the company of the Aesculapius indeed, the *gastronome* behaved like any schoolboy caught in mischief, and although the sad truth was nobody's business but his own, applied himself to disguising it. He would conceal the greater part, and present the remainder in his own way. The doctor simply raised his eyes to heaven and sighed, and Dodin understood quite well that this silent mime presaged great catastrophes. He parted from Bourboude full of heroic resolutions to settle down determinedly to green vegetables and boiled potatoes. Then, for the most fallacious reasons, he would postpone his sensible plan and, as the crisis retreated further into the past, throw upon his frugal design a daily spadeful of earth.

What happened was easy to predict. On 12 April, as Dodin inspected his spring-tide rose-bushes whilst awaiting luncheon, upon which the doctor had placed no restrictions, and which had of late acquired considerable proportions, the Master felt a shiver trickling down his left leg. His foot, suddenly leaden, became paralysed; he had the sensation that it was swelling, becoming enormous, filling the wide slipper, bursting it—that it was itself going to burst—and then the familiar cutting, burning, tearing pain settled in his big toe.

He called out loudly and had to lean upon Adèle's arm and the maid's to reach an armchair. He limped along, moaning with suffering like a small child. Sweat moistened his temples and his palms. In snatches, the doctor's sinister predictions returned to his mind half-unhinged with agony. He hopped along dragging his huge tortured foot. The act of sitting down in his dining-room, in a good armchair, of placing his leg upon another, brought him a few seconds of respite. Then the torture was resumed.

Would he send for Bourboude? Could he endure the irony in the reproachful smile he could already see upon the doctor's lips? Dodin closed his eyes; his head rolled with the rhythm of his stertorous breathing; his mouth contracted and his cheeks were drawn. . . . The two women buzzed stupidly about him, not knowing what to do.

Through the open door a slight odour of browning began to seep into the room, and, growing more and more distinct, soon became a definite smell of burned cooking. It did not escape Dodin's notice and, at the idea of scorched meat, evaporated spices, gluey sauce and lost condiments, with an imperious gesture he ordered his two inexperienced nurses to rush to the rescue of the imperilled victuals.

'But you will be left alone . . .' snivelled Adèle.

'It doesn't matter,' panted the invalid, 'the veal *matelote* will be overdone.'

He was not able to partake of the meal. Pain overwhelmed him, filling him with nausea.

He spent an atrocious day without moving from the chair or the dining-room.

Bourboude, who had hastened to his side, said not a word to him. Dodin had fully understood the eloquence of this silence. The doctor had treated his patient with devotion, but without conviction. His whole attitude expressed his impotence before the martyr's passions. He prescribed a potion intended to produce temporary relief and which in fact hardly acted at all. He had the shoe removed and the swollen foot wrapped in flannel blankets.

Dodin was sombre and fierce, tense with unaccustomed nervous energy, confronting the catastrophe which had befallen him. Until the evening he swayed to and fro, constantly turning his leg this way and that as if he wanted to shake off the pain rooted in his flesh, his breast rising and falling with the rhythm of his quickened breathing.

He inquired several times however, in an altered, languid voice, upon the state of the stuffed calves' ears and the tart of blond Bresse chicken-livers which were to be the main courses at dinner.

Eight days before he had invited his usual companions to dine with him that evening. They arrived in a group and were shown into the dining-room where the invalid received them. On many occasions, in particular at the time of Eugénie Chatagne's death, these lovers of good living had shown themselves to be ill adapted to an atmosphere of suffering in which they found it difficult to breathe.

They remained standing before the stricken *gastronome*, wide-eyed, their arms dangling, full of compassion and also of the terror that his disease might interrupt the already lengthy series of their customary revels—they shifted uneasily from one foot to the other.

Adèle opened the door to bring in the Château Chalon wine which Dodin always offered before meals : from the kitchen came such a marvellous odour that it seemed wafted from some gastronomic Olympus. In answer to this magical call, Dodin-Bouffant mastered himself.

Were not these dark hours those in which to show his friends (and tomorrow the world through which his fame was spreading) what the soul of an artist like himself was made of, and that gastronomy—the evidence and an essential part of the highest culture—contained within itself a morality that inspired energy?

He made Trifouille, Rabaz, Beaubois and Magot sit down. The thick gold of the Château Chalon was poured out for them. Then, slowly and with great effort, balancing each word against the involuntary reactions of suffering as carefully as one steps along the brink of a precipice, he began to speak.

'Do not be disturbed, my friends; enjoy peacefully and without remorse the draughts of this precious wine of our good soil which I offer you gladly. In your sparkling eyes I can see and share again the joy such nectar brings with each golden sip. It would be a sorry art that did not bequeath enough memories to re-create voluptuous pleasure, or memories too dim yet to engender perfumes. Drink, my friends. I intend to show you that pain is powerless to overcome a soul moulded by beauty which has drawn the elements of its courage from the perfection of form, sound, colour or taste. Suffering? Is it not of the same essence as rapture? Did not God wish extreme pain and pleasure to meet, and does that not convey to us a reminder that our capacity for feeling is limited; that our joys and bitternesses at bottom taste the same?'

In spite of his epicurean optimism, the sad state of his sick foot did all the same tinge Dodin's speech with melancholy.

'Suffering,' he continued, 'does not exist so long as the soul does not admit itself beaten. Whoever has conceived with himself an ideal world in which his will alone governs, can, somehow, escape from pain by taking refuge in that world. My body suffers at this moment—but my soul, flying past the smiles brought by this wine to your lips to attenuate your friendly distress, is off to the dream-gardens where our banquets are set out. . . .

Alone of the four Rabaz perceived the subtle irony of this veiled reproach. Indeed, the comforting warmth of the Château Chalon *was* helping them more easily to endure the torments of their host.

'To table, my friends,' said Dodin-Bouffant in a somewhat hoarse voice, seeing Adèle bring in the stuffed calves' ears.

They settled down expansively, comfortably spreading their napkins, knives and forks poised for the attack.

Dodin reclined by the table, but his place was not laid.

As Adèle was about to deposit the gigantic platter upon the chafing-dish, he seized it, put it before him, leaned over and resembled some pagan god in the cloud of steam which rose from the calves' ears which were full of rich stuffing and wrapped in golden breadcrumbs. He inhaled deeply, gusts of lemon and thyme, scents of fowl and sweetbreads, perfumes of broth and fresh cream; he breathed in the wine, the butter, the fat, intoxicating himself with all these varied aromas, his nostrils dilated to seize at once the whole rainbow of the symphony; his gaze ecstatic as if, released from pain, he had really eaten the magnificent dish. But, before returning to his misery, he raised severe eyes upon Adèle and said in tones of reproach:

'Your stuffing is short of half an onion and two sprigs of chervil!'

8

Dodin and the Barbarians

Neither the alarm in April, painful as it was, nor the repeated warnings of Doctor Bourboude could persuade Dodin-Bouffant to follow any but the dubious diet we described in the preceding chapter.

Not that he had forgotten the torments endured, nor that he doubted the good doctor's scientific skill, but within the rules of his art he had found a discipline which excluded all other constraints; moreover, he believed that a noble passion needed to face martyrdom before acquiring its full worth and significance. Still quivering from the abominable attack which had laid him low, he derived a sombre pleasure from defying Fate and her ugly threats.

But one morning in May, at five o'clock, Adèle woke suddenly, tortured in her turn by a violent burning pain in the left side of

her lower abdomen. Through the open door she called her husband who was sleeping peacefully, gently, in the next room. Dodin came running in his nightgown, a brilliant Madras wrapped around his head, embroidered slippers flapping on his feet, whiskers on end and still half-asleep. He found Madame Dodin-Bouffant in the grip of an acute sort of colic. She writhed continuously, jerked her body like a fish out of water, or yet again rolled over from her stomach on to her back. She groaned tirelessly, interrupting her monotonous complaint by piercing shrieks when, at regular intervals, like lighthouse signals, the pain spread sharply through her whole body. And, far from abating, the anguish grew, conquered more and more territory, and finally took up permanent residence in the kidney.

Doctor Bourboude was soon at her bedside.

'Nephritic colic,' he declared at once.

He scribbled a prescription for a laudanum enema, but after doing so, bent over Dodin-Bouffant's desk, and still holding the paper, looked up severely and said, pushing his glasses up to his forehead:

'This time, my dear sir, you are not alone involved. We must consider a woman who can expect frequent attacks of this painful nature. You are free to oppose to your own ills a stoicism which I admire as a man but condemn as a physician. But you have no right to demand of your wife the same Spartan courage. Madame Dodin-Bouffant must submit to a strict diet and spend this summer taking the waters.'

And as the doctor guessed from the sceptical expression of the *gastronome* that he had not fully succeeded in convincing him, he added:

'We are only just in time to avoid very grave consequences.'

The hour being early, and Dodin's attire somewhat negligent,

Bourboude reserved more explicit comments for the evening visit he intended to pay the patient.

When he had gone, Dodin went up to his wife. Pierrette was applying hot poultices to her anguished body, but these only soothed her momentarily. Powerless, waiting for the maid to return with the medicines she had been sent to buy, he sat down in an armchair by the window. Little by little, he awoke properly to the soft warmth of the sun, the shrill chirping of birds, the buzzing of bees and wasps starting on their rounds. He began to meditate. The poor woman emitted hideous groans, interrupted by a tremolo of squeaks and incoherent words:

'Oo—oo—ow! . . . I'm on fire . . . Oh! it's a knife in me . . . something that won't go down. . . . Oh dearie! what if I can't eat mushrooms no more? . . .'

This last interjection touched Dodin-Bouffant. By temperament, he disliked the sight of suffering, but it must also be admitted that horrible fears haunted him. Pain, when it was severe and genuine as that which gripped his wife before his eyes, irresistibly evoked the image of a grim and faithful sister—Death. And in spite of himself, the poor man could not help reliving in the past the loss of Eugénie Chatagne, the upheaval caused by her death in his own existence, the dangers his culinary art had confronted when she was gone, and the difficulty he had had in replacing that incomparable woman. . . . He wept over himself. But these vague selfish musings which passed through his brain, formless and fugitive, were followed by a more sentimental anguish, recollections of a shared life, all the flavour of an old attachment. The distress and apprehension of his heart and head mingled within him at that moment and threw him into a state of confusion.

This condition of nebulous bitterness endured for some time, but suddenly a burning flush rose to his temples and a more precise concern to the forefront of his mind: who would see to his luncheon? and his dinner? and tomorrow . . .? Adèle might be bed-ridden for several days and he would be left to the mercies of Pierrette whose education, undertaken by Madame Dodin-Bouffant, was still elementary and whose budding art owed far more to constant practice than to intuitive genius. Dodin shuddered. . . .

He did indeed lunch respectably but on fare without glory. Following his invariable custom after meals that were no more than tolerable (and how rare were these gloomy occasions in his normal life!) he locked himself in his study. Having confirmed that the patient, now calmer, was asleep, he could abandon himself to his sorrow without anxiety or remorse. Deep in his armchair, his chin low on his chest and his hands gripping the chair arms, he allowed his blank gaze to wander sadly. Now and again, he gathered his wits together to consider retrospectively all that had been lacking in the sweet-breads sauce or the chicken which had been served at luncheon, or again to seek in the mists of the past a vision of some irreproachable perfection resurrected by his palate. . . .

As the hours went by and the doctor's visit drew closer, he grew more anxious: what would Bourboude order? He had spoken of strict diet, of taking the waters. . . . A strict diet? It would then be necessary to renounce, and for ever, Adèle's inspiring by her authority and her genius the preparation of his meals and her personal supervision of their elaboration. He was too kindly, and himself too open to temptation, to exact of his wife the twice-daily self-torture of organizing his pleasures without being able to share them. So? Forever the cooking of Pierrette—alone—or another? Poor great musician condemned eternally to hear only the modest solos of a clarinet--gone the orchestra! And taking the waters? It would mean staying in some vague hotel, the regular horror of the three ready-made soup-kitchen sauces, the sapless meats, flavourless fowls and tasteless vegetables. . . . He floated in an atmosphere of despair and disaster. Minute followed minute in a chain of infinite weariness and the world seemed to have dragged itself through the last few hours at an agonized pace of collapse. He breathed in waves of distress, he drained the bitter dregs of life.

Bourboude did indeed prescribe, with the gravest and most threatening asides, a vegetarian diet as different as could be from that which Dodin had devised for his evening meals. Then he raised the question of a watering-place: Baden-Baden was becoming fashionable, and its waters, glorified by this budding popularity, were believed capable of curing any and every disease.

'It is absolutely urgent,' peremptorily affirmed the Aescula-pius, 'that Madame Dodin-Bouffant should go there for a strict cure. And you too, my dear Sir, would do well to undergo treat-ment at the same time. A season of the waters cannot fail to do you the greatest good.'

The scent of great burgundies miraculously filled the olfactive memory of the *gastronome*, while his mouth contorted itself in a premature grimace at the putrid flavour of sulphurous water.

Several more attacks and the tenacious insistence of Bourboude were needed to make Dodin, at the beginning of June, resolve firmly to leave with his spouse for the Grand Duchy. He had already decided upon the trip several times, when a slight twinge reminded him of his foot or his wife's kidneys. But each warning over, he would gaze tenderly at his sun-kissed, flowering garden, his comfortable house, and then at Adèle to whose appearance his compatriots were accustomed but who could not fail to be conspicuous in an elegant spa, and his decision would collapse into utter apathy.

They reserved a chaise for 27 June. Dodin left the packing to Adèle, taking upon himself only the task of filling a large carpet-bag with gastronomic books, the savoury reading of which was to console him for a reality which he anticipated with fear. He also included in his personal luggage a stout flask of *lie-de-raisin*. For so many years he had never spent more than a couple of days away from his county, his friends, his house, and the night before their departure he slept very little. In his mind he turned over the thought in which he still hoped to find an imperative and decisive pretext for withdrawal: namely that the 'cure' with its attendant hardships upon which they were about to embark would hasten, more surely than any uric or gout attacks endured at home, the irreparable ruin of their health and the end of their good life together.

He no longer dared to retreat, however, now that the public adieux had been made, the coach ordered, the hotel rooms reserved, and the whole village had gossiped for a fortnight over this momentous departure. But he was tormented by doubts. He foresaw carriages wrecked in ditches; in his imagination he tasted the infamous waters to be forced down their throats. He could see himself, swollen to suffocation point beside an Adèle gurgling with the sound of an ever-flowing inner cascade, both of them weakened by the noxious liquid so that they could not travel home, condemned to end their days in dropsical ruin crawling about the depths of the German duchy. Worst of all, he thought of the deplorable food in shameful inns; he smelled the stale echoes of grease and slops, the stench of coarse, popular frying and sickening stews. Madame Dodin-Bouffant, more practical and less imaginative, snored peacefully in the next room.

The first birdsong made the poor epicure shiver: it sounded weird and funereal. The hour drew near, and now that he must leave them, his place, his familiar possessions took on a fresh charm which he had never noticed, enhanced by the new melancholy atmosphere. For the first time, on the point of leaving it, he truly saw the setting of his own life.

Beaubois, Magot, Rabaz, Trifouille and Doctor Bourboude surrounded the unhappy couple by the carriage. Like novices advancing full of fear and respect towards a grave and mysterious ceremony, Monsieur and Madame Dodin-Bouffant had dressed for the voyage in formal garments: grey velvet top hat, puce frilled dress, lace scarf, gold-buttoned frock-coat, pipe-stem trousers and Leghorn straw garlanded in silk flowers. They were encumbered with a thousand parcels, bags, bundles, suit-cases and umbrellas. Before mounting the high carriage-step, Adèle gave Pierrette and the snivelling maid-servant her final instructions. At last, their friends saw the travellers installed in the carriage, leaning back against the comfortable little mattress of rose-printed cretonne, looking infinitely woebegone. The vehicle moved off in a symphony of creaks and hoofbeats and a whirlwind of dust.

As long as they were driving through France, the voyage was comparatively pleasant. The couple dozed to the swing of the tall springs, emerging only at meal-times from the oblivion induced by emotion, vague anguish and monotonous movement. They had tacitly agreed that being in exceptional circumstances, and moreover about to receive treatment which must cure them, there was no point in their following a diet prescribed for normal conditions. Dinners and luncheons were therefore generously inclusive of meat, fish and wine. The element of surprise in staging-post meals, in wayside inn cookery, amused and entertained them. Besides, everywhere they found comfortable food which, whilst it did not attain the complete perfection of their family fare, had its own charm. At its own supremely high level, Dodin's taste had acquired through its very sublimity, a certain good-humoured indulgence. Indeed, certain local dishes, certain indigenous manners of preparing meals, completely charmed the Master; he acknowledged their worth most willingly and went so far as to ask for the recipes. At such times all his lyrical verve returned to him as he enjoyed and analysed everything. His speech, once again, was fluent and free. An unexpected wine would bring back his cheerfulness and his joie-de-vivre. The scented breath of ancient bottles, the flavours of palatable and carefully-blended meats, mingled in him to reawaken and cheer his soul.

'You know, Adèle,' he would say, 'travel is a good thing all the same. One enlarges the scope of one's knowledge, one learns, one appreciates new delights. . . .'

Adèle listened without much show of comprehension but ate and drank mightily as a connoisseur and a practician. Her mood responded exactly to the flights and falls of her Lord and Master's.

Then they would return to the carriage. Meadows, streams, valleys again rolled past the windows. They agreed to find these less rich, less pure and less fresh than the meadows, streams and valleys of their own little land from which each wheel-turn took them farther. They felt lost—strangers in far countries . . . discomfort descended upon them . . . digestion took its toll, and they closed their eyes until the next meal.

In spite of the wise slowness which Dodin decreed for the voyage, they must eventually reach the frontiers of the kingdom. There, the gourmet drew himself up: they were about to step on to foreign soil, an event which, for this man of sedentary habits who had not for thirty years gone farther than the Vaudois and Genevese villages bordering his own province, took on the most precise gravity and seemed pregnant with vague dangers. As head of the family, he owed it to his mate to be fully master of himself and of the situation, to protect her against possible peril. He straightened his back, pulled down the flowered nankeen waistcoat over his imposing belly, adjusted his hat, and tucked some of his watch-chain into his pocket. Thus equipped, suspicious but magnificent, he confronted the Customs' Officers of His Excellency the Grand Duke of Baden. The disagreeable ceremony over—and Dodin submitted to it in a disdainful silence—the travellers noticed outside the office buildings a long table in the middle of which stood a vast cauldron over a small stove. Around this steaming centrepiece were piles of plates, mounds of black bread, and a multitude of earthenware bowls.

The arrival of the mail-coach soon satisfied the couple's curiosity about the contents of the cauldron at which they gazed with foreign uncertainty. A pretty, blonde young woman of ethereal appearance though somewhat too rosy complexion, with dreamy, blue-innocent eyes, rushed over as soon as the step was lowered. A chubby giant of a cook lifted the lid of the container and the poetic Gretchen, pushing back her organdie sleeves from delicate, blue-veined wrists, seized in her dainty fingers a pair of plump sausages from which dripped boiling water. Holding a large piece of bread in the other hand, she began to chew heartily on the *würstchen* which crackled under her teeth, releasing from their little split skins a stream of hot fat which ran down to anoint her chin with glistening varnish. Two more, and yet two more sausages, again accompanied by wholemeal bread, followed the first pair. Several earthenware bowls of heavy beer washed down these larded, fat pork morsels.

Dodin-Bouffant and Adèle observed this feast with astonishment. It was but ten in the morning, and evidently this generous collation was only intended to whet the frail young person's appetite for her midday meal. The gourmet conceived for her a strange respect, mingled with the disgust he felt at the mask of grease which disfigured her. However, he decided to try for himself those sausages which, coarse as they appeared, filled the air with a not unpleasant odour of smoked meats. Although it revolted him to eat them with his fingers, he made the effort. But suddenly he paled and frowned heavily, seeming to swell up disproportionately in his attempt to swallow the imprudent mouthful, whilst he tried with a convulsive gesture, to protect his frock-coat from the flow of accursed hot grease already polluting his well-shaven cheeks, his impeccable chin, and trickling along his well-groomed hand and wrist, burning him as it invaded his cuff. Hastily, though not without dignity, he placed upon the table some local money which he had just changed, threw the remains of the sausages to the groom's dog, and whilst still trying to free his jaws from the glue-paste of the black bread, drew Adèle towards their carriage where he barricaded himself, severe and outraged, against the malign influences which he felt surrounded them.

Luncheon at the next stage made the Master shudder. Haughty, reserved and full of suspicion, he sat with Adèle at a remote corner of the *table d'hôte*. But his presence and magnificent size caused him, in fact, to preside. The dishes were brought to him first, and with what ironic serenity, for just one second, he would look at them and shake his head that they might be removed from his sight! With the first course he understood fully—saw everything crystal-clear. On a gigantic dish lay an omelet of uncommon proportions from the overcooked sides of which trickled threads of melted cheese, whilst around the scorched monster a pink and sweetish-looking jelly trembled piteously. All around the table, jaws began to champ and noisy suckings attempted to seize together the slippery cheese omelet and the escaping gooseberry jelly. It was utterly nauseating. Dodin-Bouffant saw a huge mug overflowing with iced beer firmly deposited before him. . . . He closed his eyes and saw, in a mist of glory, wearing human features and reproaching him in gentle silence, the old bottles of his cellar, the friendly flasks of precious wines, all those aristocratic vintages, so noble and delicate, so warm and varied. Adèle, famished and less heroic than her husband, had tried to taste the omelet, helping herself from the centre in an attempt to avoid the noisome jelly. But from the first mouthful her refined taste had discerned the burnt flavour of a mixture both tough and soggy, accompanied by that of an imitation tenth-rate gruyère. She put down her fork and, stupefied by sorrow and astonishment, allowed her childish old eyes to wander over the noisy swollen business-man, the shiny young woman, the doll-like old grey-beard, the commercial traveller with the fierce eyes, all of whom were savouring the abomination with intense enjoyment. She resolved to let herself die of starvation.

Dodin barely put his lips to the large radishes prepared with sauerkraut. The grease in which they had been cooked made the dish atrocious, but the Master imagined that one might, with ingenious preparation, achieve something worth while with this variety of vegetable which was new to him. The goose-fillets which he and Adèle accepted (supreme idea and supreme optimism!) drew a double grunt from them: stringy and oily they were from a very elderly bird doubtless nourished upon wholemeal, left-overs and greasy water.

The appetites around them seemed whetted by each course. Admiring murmurs and interjections burst from those bulging gluttons. Some of them, replete and gasping, sighed out gusty mystical invocations: 'Ach Gott! . . .' mixing the name of God with the dreadful food in their mouths. The Emperor of Gastronomy groaned sadly. Leaning back in his chair, his hands folded upon his vast belly, he had assumed the air of a man who definitely renounces food. He was resigned. By then, in any case, his body had ceased to exist in the present . . . he was seated in his own dining-room . . . helping Rabaz to a partridge in aspic . . . upon the table stood a pie in which a pounded shrimp sauce enhanced the golden chicken-livers . . . in each glass, before each guest, a ruby star twinkled in the soft light. . . .

Settling in at the sign of the Black Ram at Baden-Baden was most laborious. To the exile, everything seemed hostile and inconvenient: the drawers that stuck or squeaked, the chairs so inhospitable to his own harmonious rotundity, the harsh coarse towels that smelled of yellow soap. They arrived at a late hour, and imprisoned as he was in prohibitions, alas too well-founded, Dodin ordered for his wife and himself a light supper to be served in their rooms: eggs, ham, salad. He ate, for the first time in his life, without paying the slightest attention to this necessary and instinctive operation. He was not hungry: both of them were tired out, desperate and disgusted.

In the morning he summoned the Manager.

'Sir,' he said to him with a touch of ironic pride, 'you may not know of me. In my country, my compatriots have seen fit to grant me a certain competence in the difficult art of the table. I have made a profound study of gastronomy. . . .'

The hotelier bowed automatically in a series of deep inclinations.

'Ach, Herr Doktor . . .'

'No—not Doctor—*gastronome*, quite simply. I am accustomed to particularly excellent cookery. Madame'—he pointed to Adèle—'is an outstanding artist who is good enough to survey my fare. It is of her that the Prince of Eurasia used to say . . .'

At the sound of this magnificent name, the innkeeper again began to bow and scrape, but this time with heels clicking together, at attention so to speak, with the most profound deference.

'I therefore ask you to make especially sure that our table should be composed of dishes of the best quality, lengthily, lovingly, carefully prepared. That everything should be simple, but perfect.'

And as the manager poured out a thousand assurances and protestations, Dodin, impatiently, began to shave.

Though but scantily reassured by his own demands and the assurances of the hotelier that his establishment fully satisfied the familiars of foreign courts, exceedingly rich Americans, the British nobility and the most exacting Russians, Dodin took the arm of his faithful companion for whom, through their trials and tribulations, his admiration was growing into veneration, and allowed himself to enjoy the pleasures of discovering a new country. Well-kept lawns, groves of shady trees, fresh springs in the park, all struck him as having a charm of their own. As age had not attenuated his appetite for pretty women—on the contrary—he was pleasurably stirred by the sight of the attractive bathers who brightened the pump rooms and the casino.

From the whole world came the most fashionable and elegant of women to this most fashionable and elegant spa, and Dodin, long immured in his provincial fastnesses and limited to purely imaginary satisfaction of his taste for love, began to cheer up considerably. It was in excellent spirits that he sat down to the table d'hôte of the Black Ram. But a small cloud brushed his good-humour as he entered the dining-room. The shrill quavering sound of guitars floated from this sanctuary where, according to his lights, nothing, not even picturesque music, should disturb the august hour. Then too he was greeted by a crowd of obsequious flunkeys dressed with an elegance which almost made him ashamed of his own simple and correct garb. However, being seated beside a very beautiful Italian lady who did not seem to mind exchanging sidelong glances, he continued to feel indulgently disposed towards the cooking. Adèle was literally crushed by the splendour of her surroundings. The elaborate mouldings, the abundance of mirrors, the silver-gilt cutlery, the black marble clock filled her with immense admiration and left her breathless, although she felt instinctively that such blatant luxury rarely promises serious cuisine. Dodin, however, still absorbed in his pretty neighbour, was abruptly brought back to a more earnest view of things. At a separate table, but not far from him, five people, three men and two women, were speaking English rather loudly. No doubt these were some of the noble strangers of whom the innkeeper had boasted and whom he had quoted as considering his cuisine excellent. Well-groomed, distinguished-looking, correct, the Master thought they must be at least Lords or transatlantic millionaires. . . . What would he see brought to these aristocrats, no doubt accustomed in their sumptuous homes to unimaginable daily wonders? What unexpected treasures, what delicate and studied dishes would be reserved for them? A waiter arrived bearing an immense tray. He placed six dishes on the gentlemen's table: a veal stew, boiled potatoes, spinach, sausages, chunks of smoked eel, and a chocolate pudding. And Dodin saw, with his own eyes saw, the Anglo-Saxons spear upon nimble forks or spoon up deftly pieces, portions, sections of each dish, pile these indiscriminately upon their plates, and eat together the entrée, the meat, the vegetables and the dessert. . . . They moistened this terrifying mixture with copious draughts of iced water. A shudder seized the nape of his neck and spread painfully down his back, like a thousand ants. That there should be on earth beings of human appearance who could feed like that and drink water was already prodigious and unbelievable. But it was none of his business. In the four days of his journey he had been obliged to temper his own utter intransigence with much resignation. He was getting blasé. But what *was* his business, however, was the infamous soup-kitchen to be inferred from the foreigners' . . . fodder. If the hotel-keeper had given the taste of these people as a reference, what could he not expect to see upon his own plate! And besides, in an hotel with culinary traditions to uphold, would it have been permissible to serve guests with such appalling eating-habits?

He was brought a hollow dish, full of a sticky sauce of indefinite colour, in which, as in greyish varnish, swam massive meat-balls. With infinite care he tasted . . . and was immediately choked by a paste of hash and flour, dried sultanas, and soaked in a porridge of Madeira from a cheap wineshop. It filled and immobilized his mouth like gum or wet plaster, the pepper burning him, and a thousand nauseous flavours poisoning his palate. He turned green and only avoided returning the mouthful to his plate by a heroic display of good manners. To recover himself, he drank a long draught of Rhenish wine which however he did not like because it was far too cold and excessively scented. Next came a *Rehbraten*, a poor roast of venison, not only totally lacking in the wild succulence which constitutes the charm of game, but also impregnated with a taste of urine which had not been drained after the kill, and—supreme disgrace!—innocent of the least preparatory marinade. On the other hand, it was lavishly garnished with a sauce in which sour cream and flour mingled with the gravy. The accompanying prunes did little to enhance this melancholy product of the chase.

'Adèle,' he said in a tone of indescribable sadness, 'I do not feel very well. I am going up to our rooms.'

The sorrow that hollowed her husband's eyes and pinched his nostrils was so immense that Adèle dared not affront it. She wanted to give him time to master himself in solitude. So she remained there at table, poor, fat, lost thing, surrounded by sonorous mastication, pomeranian mirth, uncontrolled verbiage. . . .

She found Dodin crumpled up in his armchair. He mopped a damp brow, his eyes floundering in infernal visions of future meals. . . . He threw her a dying glance, full of all human anguish, and tenderly taking her hand, with the gesture of a man who has suffered greatly and weeps over himself:

'It is very true, as Montaigne says in the *Voyages*, that these Germans "provide far finer plate and china than do our hostelries in France", but, Dear Lord who created all Good and all Beauty, what do they put in it! '

From then on Dodin ate no more at the Black Ram. He began to explore and to test, in search of comparatively Christian nourishment, the hotels, inns and restaurants of Baden-Baden and the surrounding country. His first indignation past, he maintained a dignified severity of demeanour. He tasted —he tasted again and yet again—tirelessly tasted all the Teutonic rubbish offered to him which confirmed in every way his opinion of the heaviness, the lack of taste, and the prodigious stomach of the subjects of Prussia and their confederates. From scornful lips he allowed severe judgements to fall upon them. Beside him, as counsellor in his majestic court, Adèle approved, and frequently embroidered upon those judgements in energetic and picturesque terms which she had not abandoned to the kitchen on her promotion to the dining-room, and which Dodin-Bouffant pretended not to hear. Sometimes he would express his own dismay in gentler terms : faced with a stringy and tasteless *Gansebraten*, for instance, swimming in the eternal creamy but brackish sauce which monotonously accompanied pretentious insipidities, he murmured to himself, opposing two aspects of the indigenous soul in one lapidary formula :

'My God! What *can* that poor Werther have eaten ?'

However, guided by instinct, upheld by tireless perseverance, and at last favoured by fortune, Dodin did gradually discover, here and there, after patient searching, certain local specialities pleasant enough to ensure his survival. Behind the bathing establishment, a papier-mâché medieval inn known as the Horseshoe served a fruity Alsatian wine, perhaps a trifle rough, but original and full of personality. At the end of the promenade, by the town gates, the Grand Ducal Brasserie's smoked goose-breast was excellent. A pastryshop offered the solace of very tolerable jam-puffs, and one could always be sure of finding some cheerful cold-pork with horse-radish, or a delicately flavoured liver-sausage at the tiny third-rate hotel called the Black Forest.

Lacking anything better, Dodin knew how to live off the land. The doctor attached to the establishment had prescribed a

suitable diet for the couple. Adèle, still upset by her recent sufferings, obeyed fairly scrupulously. As for the Master, after two days of loyal efforts he had evolved an ingenious system, a compromise between instinct and good sense, which most harmoniously married the requirements of health and the imperative demands of taste.

Towards nine he would tramp down to the springs and drink (with many grimaces, holding his breath) of the waters. His eyes showed through the glass, dilated with horror at the beverage he was constrained to swallow, blushing with shame. As the doctor had advised him to let an interval of forty-five minutes elapse between each absorption of water—he was condemned to three of these—without specifying what he was to do in the intervals, as soon as he had done his irksome duty he would hasten blissfully to the Horseshoe, settle himself upon a garden bench, and order a bottle of Alsatian wine. Then, after three quarters of an hour, he would return to the torture-chamber, and thence, very shortly, to his pleasure. In this manner he drank three glasses of the waters every morning, and three bottles of wine. Neither Adèle nor the doctor could convince him that serious treatment included only the first part of his programme.

One afternoon at five o'clock, on his return from a constitutional, the hall-porter brought to their room where Adèle was already resplendent in a prune-coloured satinette wrapper and curl-papers, a visiting card:

Prof. Dokt. Hugo STUMM
Geheimrat
Philosophischer Schriftsteller.

Although somewhat surprised Dodin-Bouffant said to show the visitor in. A tall man appeared, fairly heavily built, mopping away at a bony brow from which an obstinate dew seemed reluctant to depart. Spectacles tightly anchored to his ears and apparently screwed into the bridge of his nose formed an integral part of his face. That nose, moreover, was half as long as ordinary noses, terminating in a prodigious flat width in the centre of a round face. The mouth, between massive jaws, had far less of a human appearance than that of an artificial cement-mixer. His cranium was outlined by a regular but choppy shadow which did duty for very short-cropped hair.

Upon the threshold the professor began to greet Monsieur and Madame Dodin-Bouffant with bows from the waist alone— leaving the rest of his anatomy quite motionless except his heels which clicked together monotonously. Then he began, in a French that trickled drop by drop:

'I have just, of the stay here of the illustrious Dodin-Bouffant, the friend of the Prince of Eurasia (here he sketched in empty space a salute to the absent monarch), learned. That the very noble lady Madame Dodin-Bouffant to present myself allow me should. . . .'

Adèle was flabbergasted, her curl-papered head like a ship full-dressed, legs apart, and comb in hand, swaying like her loose wrapper, and carried off unwittingly by the professor's example, returned, stroke for stroke, with clumsy gestures of head and shoulders, the solemn bows of the visitor.

'Professor Doktor Hugo Stumm, Geheimrat, Philosophischer Schriftsteller . . . first lieutenant of the Landwehr, brother of Prussian Guard Captain Otto Stumm. . . .'

Dodin, tired and somewhat footsore after his walk, gestured to the professor to take a seat, sat down himself, and wishing to conform to the manners of the country, said simply:

'Allow me, Sir, Brother of the Captain of the Guard, the

Prussian Guard, Otto Stumm, to remove my shoes and put on my slippers.' With the awkwardness of the obese in bending, he removed one shoe. Hugo Stumm had begun:

'I come to speak to you, *berühmter Herr Professor*, of the metaphysic of cooking which is my special subject.' (The reader will forgive us for not reproducing all the Teutonic inversions of verbs which added to the puzzlement upon Dodin-Bouffant's face as he stood up, one sock on and one in his hand.) The great man's expression could not be misread even by Stumm who, feeling somewhat embarrassed, decided to explain more clearly.

'I have already written the one thousand seven hundred and eight-three first pages of an essentially hegelio-platonic work, the title of which is *The Metaphysics of Cookery*.'

A vague shudder, a dizziness, shook Adêle. In her muddled brain a collision took place between the barbarous word 'metaphysics' and the vision of saucepans inevitably conjured up by the word 'cookery', and she trembled lest the stranger might not have slighted her beloved art in some obscure way. However, she was reassured by her husband's calm. Stumm resumed:

'It will be nothing new to you, illustrious Master, if I state the principle that cookery in itself, like everything else in the world, is no more than an illusion of our senses. Only the Idea that springs from it has any real value.'

Dodin rolled his eyes, his expression conveyed doubts of the German's sanity, his irritation, and his suspicion of sharp practice, whilst ineffable memories, quite unconnected with the Idea, protested within him at the bold statement. The other continued placidly:

'I must describe to you the plan of my book and its basic Ideas.'

He twisted his hat incessantly between pudgy fingers, the stupid gesture underlining his complete self-satisfaction.

'So. Only the Idea of Cookery is important. I have devoted my life to proving this, and have now reached the stage when I consume only boiled potatoes and cabbage-water. . . .'

'*How* I understand you!' exclaimed Dodin, remembering the meat-balls.

The other took this exclamation to be approving, and continued:

'Since you approve these premisses, we must now undertake a transcendental analysis of my Idea. Stripped of all the artifice bestowed upon it by our needs, of all the superfluity with which our deliquescence has adorned it, let us take it first of all in its original simplicity: the Idea of cookery is simply one of the essential forms taken by our vital instinct, of our will to live. The typical cook is the most ancient man of prehistory, whose skill was limited to removing from a bleeding auroch's quarter those portions too tough to chew. His son, by placing this joint amidst flaming branches, had already moved away from the pure Idea. In the platonic world, the Idea of cookery is linked quite simply with the other great abstraction of the vital instinct: the Idea of Reproduction.'

Dodin, dazed, remained quite still, holding his shoe. His raised head, his extended arm, had not moved at all.

'You have certainly noticed, honoured Master, that the Idea of reproduction, throughout the centuries, has constantly recurred in the human brain. With the exception of certain degenerates who are, I regret to state, almost exclusively to be found in your country, and who have substituted for the primordial act unhealthy excitements which have finally swallowed up the act itself, excitements which, I observe with the same regret, have not failed greatly to alter the relationships of the sexes in your country; with the exception of these few degenerates, I say, and of their disciples, humanity continues to reproduce itself by the same primitive gesture, and in this manner the pure Idea and its material aspect have remained pretty well unchanged.'

This lengthy phrase wrenched a small grunt of pain from the gastronome.

'The same cannot be said of cookery: greed which shortly after man's appearance on earth vitiated and complicated the simple wish to survive, has everywhere replaced this original need, and today the elaborate cookery of civilized peoples is as different from primitive nourishment as. . . .'

'As Black Forest meat-balls from artistic gastronomy,' growled Dodin-Bouffant, whose blood was coming to the boil. He put down his shoe at last. Hugo Stumm did not appear to hear his interruption, or else, absorbed in his argument, did not understand it. He went on:

'These are well-founded premisses, I believe. Now you know, of course, Herr Doktor, that the whole Universe, with frenzied and painful efforts, tends to co-ordinate its scattered parts and to rebuild itself in Unity, or rather the Unities of the world of Ideas. It is a fact. Everything which gravitates towards simple Unity consequently escapes the strangle-hold of Matter and returns to its Ideal origins. That is why every philosopher must unreservedly approve the traditional policy of our Hohenzollerns who, pursuing the unification of Germany (under their sceptres) throughout the centuries . . . then the unification of Europe, and finally that of the world, have established themselves firmly within the logic of metaphysical order.

'But I return to cookery, and it is from the point of view which I have had the honour of outlining to you, that I shall consider the subject. Its greatest living apostle, the successor of Apicius, of Diodomus of Alicante, of Remus Variconus, of Aristobal, of

Eumenius Scartey, and of so many others, cannot but appreciate the magnitude of my attempt to raise his art or his science to the speculative sphere of the Spirit.'

Dodin, appalled by such eloquence but not a little impressed by the display of an unfamiliar erudition, had finally decided to undergo these assaults in the comfort of the armchair in which, until then, he had appeared to be but temporarily ensconced— torn between his desire to end the interview and the respect which he felt in spite of everything for the charlatan.

'The human effort which will extract cookery from the rut of materialism and set it upon the road of the Spirit consists there- fore in uprooting this unhealthy diversity and introducing into its disorder and complexity the elements which must bring it back to primitive Unity, to the light of the Idea! Therefore, we must simplify, simplify utterly, reaccustom our faculties of taste to the few rudimentary flavours, protect them from depraving research, from decadent mixtures, offer them ever more normal satisfactions—that is to say cruder ones, and thus plan for the day when cookery, once more only an element of man's vital instinct, will limit itself to maintaining life, to preparing pieces of raw meat as did our ancestors.'

'It seems to me,' Dodin mumbled between set teeth, 'that your compatriots and certain Americans of my acquaintance are well on that road already. . . .'

'In this way cookery will have completed its Platonic cycle and have become the most magnificent, the most metaphysical of the arts. Starting from the Unity of the Idea, it will have realized its full awareness by passing through all the stages of diversity and returning, through them, to original Unity. From the clear vision of this destiny, I draw the rules, the laws, which must inspire the dominant masters who practise and guide cookery, and with them, all human beings with brains and will-power.

'In one spiritual field at least, Man, by abolishing the artificial categories in his mind, will no longer obey anything but the categorical imperative to reach, behind or through those artificialities of appearance, the Reality of Things! We shall then have extracted from Cookery that Imperative from which we cannot escape.'

After a certain silence which confirmed Dodin's hope that the speech had at last come to an end, he rose, and placing his hands behind his back, began to pace up and down the room without even noticing Adèle who had collapsed under the monstrous philosophical nonsense which Hugo Stumm had dared to stir up in her saucepans. Dodin remained silent for some minutes. The philosopher, still twisting his hat between his hands, wriggled joyfully upon his chair, anticipating enthusiastic approval, and never doubting his conquest by reasoning of the illustrious friend of the Prince of Eurasia. From this important conversion he anticipated a thousand helpful consequences. At last, still pacing, Dodin let fall the following words:

'Sir, Brother of the Landwehr Captain Otto Stumm' (and this time he imbued the phrase with all the insolence his sensual lips could convey), 'one of my friends—she died on the scaffold during the Revolution—the pretty Madame de Lassuze, when d'Alembert explained to her the doctrines of your Kant, replied to him: 'All the Imperatives in the world weigh nothing against a sin committed for tenderness.' And I think that your metaphysician, and all your metaphysics as well, are—excuse me, Madame Bouffant—blasted to bits by those simple words. All your Idea of Cookery is a dog's dinner against a shrimp sauce, or a Dombes wild duck, or the "Pillow of Beautiful Dawn" of my divine friend, M. Brillat Savarin, who wrote "Animals feed; man eats. Only the superior man knows how to eat." Those twelve words utterly demolish your nonsense, if it ever had sufficient solidity to be demolished.'

Dodin looked so imperious that Stumm, crushed, did not even try to protest.

'But I am not surprised that the folly of reducing cookery to a pure Idea, embodied moreover in a quarter of raw meat, should have occurred in this country. Certainly your national nourishment would gain thereby, Sir. Do not, however, hope that any citizen of my country would understand a single word of your so-called philosophy, let alone subscribe to it. *We* invented preserved goose, mushroom *ragoût*, chicken in cream, truffles with bacon, chicken-liver pies, royal hare, shrimp puffs, *we* did, Sir, and so many other things! We have Burgundy, Bordeaux and Anjou, *we* have, Sir, for if I understand you rightly, it is spring water you would offer us to wash down the bloody raw meat and thus satisfy the pure Idea of Thirst! It would be too simple, Sir, to rejoin that thanks to a natural philosophy of far greater nobility, far greater authority than the little job you have tried to construct, we use the gifts that God has given us. It would seem that the Divinity, which is the Idea of Ideas, has not sown upon our poor earth a thousand delicate treasures in order that we should feed on quarters of raw meat. You may not have given this detail any thought. Your theory is therefore built upon a stupid misconception, as is, moreover, the whole of your philosophy which, by attempting to reverse the immutable terms of the problem, has always wished to deduce metaphysic from a moral precept.'

Hugo Stumm made a final attempt to interrupt. If he could take fairly equably the criticism addressed to himself, this destruction in one stroke of all German philosophy was intolerable.

'Wait, Sir,' said Dodin-Bouffant severely, 'for *I* have listened patiently to *you.*

'Though it has no place in your metaphysical order, and refuses such a place, what nobility, what greatness and what clarity there are in the cookery of my country, a cookery which consists, I assure you, neither of Pure Idea nor of raw meat. I can tell you—but how would you judge?—that it has no need of your foggy reasoning nor your ponderous periods to rise, like Phaeton, to glory and the sun. Grace and refinement, blending and proportion, exact measure and sure taste carry within them their own virtue; when their fortunate union succeeds in raising man above himself, in exalting him and bearing him to heights far beyond his own human condition, they achieve a fullness of effect which makes them irresistible, sovereign and ideal forces. Can you even dimly suspect how grotesque it would be for us to sterilize the Idea and pound it into the purplish fibres of raw meat when, as sons of the great Pascal, the wonderful Rabelais, the wise Montaigne, we wish, as we enjoy the whole world on our forks, to fill that Idea with all the breath and enthusiasm of Life itself?

'Sir, we have no more to say to each other.'

9

Return and Resolution

━━━━◼◖◉◗◼◖◉◗◼◖❋◗◼◖◉◗◼◖◉◗◼━━━━

On 2 October, the young Bressane peasant-girl appointed to look after the Dodin-Bouffant household during the couple's absence received a letter in which they announced their return on the 17th of that month. She was instructed—instructions accompanied by three pages of detailed recipes and prescriptions—to prepare for that day a broth made from old fowls, tongue, and a skirt of beef, from parsnips, turnips, carrots and celery; to have on hand well-concentrated beef glaze, extract of fresh mushrooms, a fine veal kidney—the colour, weight and right quantity of fat were exactly described—to remove the white meat from a turkey, blanch twelve chicken-livers, obtain six dozen fine prawns, and finally to write to Lavanchy at Bulle for a good fat piece of authentic Gruyère to be delivered at the right time. In addition, she was to place three bottles of Château-Chalon on ice not later than six o'clock in the morning, and bring as many flasks of Vergelesses to room temperature.

'As for the rest,' added Adèle Pidou, 'don't worry about anything: I shall officiate in person.'

An hour after the arrival of this missive the whole little town had learned of the Master's impending return. Emotions immediately rose to a peak in cafés, bourgeois homes, the club, the market, the staging-inn. It had so greatly been feared that the voyage might be fatal to the great man—that only his corpse would be brought back to be laid beside that of Eugénie Chatagne! A mood of relaxed joyousness swept over the city when the good news was spread by the little maidservant who was proud to be the bearer of glad tidings.

Ah! how long the time seemed to Dodin-Bouffant's compatriots until the day their hero had elected to return to them!

Magot, Beaubois, Rabaz and Trifouille met daily to anticipate the joy of that blessed hour when the stage-coach would appear at the top of the hill and enter the town. They would first reassure each other that none of them had received any bad news or learned of an accident or a contretemps since their last meeting, and then give themselves up once again to their proud pleasure, their glory, in being the intimate friends of the expert gourmet: had they not the right to be more affected than anyone by the return of the great man which stirred the whole city?

At last 17 October dawned. It was an exceptionally brilliant and warm day, a day to gladden the heart. You would have thought it the King's birthday, there was so much gay loitering and unaccustomed strolling about in autumnal sunshine. Some lads sent out as scouts watched for the carriage in the direction of the Tuilieries, at the mouth of the valley. All who had been able to leave their office, workshop or store, drifted to the city gates, or sat on the grass or in the inns, waiting. . . .

153

Towards two o'clock, at last, the scouts arrived running, followed quite soon by the muffled sound of regular hoofbeats.

'Here they come, here they come!' they cried breathlessly tired, dusty and sweating like Marathon runners.

In a flash the crowd was lined up on either side of the road. Brief snatches of talk mingled with others: 'In what state will they be, mon Dieu! . . . What a lucky escape! . . . Poor Dodin, poor Adèle! . . . What will the Barbarians have done to them? . . .'

The carriage appeared and passed on at a measured pace, as if the *gastronome*'s placid and thoughtful soul had affected even the demeanour of the horses. It moved on in the midst of murmured respect and affection, hats dropping before it like corn before the sickle. At that moment Dodin-Bouffant, miraculously returning safe and sound from faraway, fabulous lands, re-entered his home town like those legendary heroes of whose worth, works or exploits nothing is known any longer, but in whom a whole population enshrines its instinct for glory. The great man was back! From the upholstered depths of the vehicle, relishing the unexpected homage of his compatriots, he began to forget his recent trials. Beside him, Adèle, puffed out like a pouter-pigeon, tried hard to arrange her emaciated features, emerging from a tangled organdie collar and a Paisley shawl, into a suitable expression of dignity.

The disciples awaited them on the porch of the little house. The young Bressane stood with them, incapable of expressing her emotion save by thumping her stomach and her thighs and wiping away her tears.

The members of the little circle, who had noticeably put on weight while the Master faced the perils we have described, received him with open arms. At the first glance at their paunches

Dodin noted, not without mortification, the advantages of not rushing about the world's highways; it did not escape their notice, either, that the waistcoat of their master no longer exactly moulded his powerful belly. His legs seemed unsteady and his face looked worn and furrowed by fatigue. . . . But a joyous light, full of promise, shone in his eyes as they wandered in relieved enchantment over his home and his old friends. He embraced them all, choked by a holy emotion.

As for Adèle, she minced down the carriage steps, shaking out the folds and frills of her pigeons' wing silk dress, like a lady traveller who has escaped from great dangers and contemplated what vulgar eyes will never see. Then she disappeared. The five friends only found, in Dodin's study which she had passed through like a draught, her vanity bag, her mittens and her overnight case. But from the neighbouring kitchen they heard her imperious, vigorous voice and those thousand precise, assured noises which accompany the activity of a diligent and competent cook.

'The good soul!' murmured Dodin-Bouffant. 'Without even taking a few minutes to go up to her room she has started on my evening meal! She wants our first dinner on our return to wipe out the memory of that abominable cure!'

The friends settled down comfortably in the good old familiar armchairs. Dodin sent for the three bottles of an authentic Madeira which, forty years before, a friend who alas had since died, brought back to him in one of his company's ships. He was surprised to see the venerable flasks on a japanned tray dominating a whole landscape of kirsch flans which Adèle had hastily concocted for their collation. The afternoon seemed delicious to the epicure emerging from his Germanic Gehenna. His soul settled into its accustomed place among his old books, his old friends, his old furniture; and his legs, tired of ceremonial wear, slid into the familiar folds of shapeless trousers with relief.

The book he had been handling before setting out—*l'Almanach des Gourmands* by the Comte de Périgord—was still there upon his table. How many painful adventures, how many bitter moments, how many sinister experiences he had had since last he turned its pages!

He minutely questioned his disciples about the events in the town since his departure. But whenever one or the other of them tried to interrogate him about his voyage, he closed his eyes as if he could not endure the horrid visions that sprang up before them. He brought the conversation back to the town, *their* town, insisting upon detailed descriptions of their menus, flavours of dishes which interested him, a dinner the landlady of the Café de Saxe had prepared for them, a supper at the Deputy Prefect's. . . . Visibly, he shunned the terrifying memory of the weeks he had just lived through. His friends quickly understood that they must not inflict upon him the suffering of evoking them.

Then, with the close of day, the last flans and the ultimate drops of Madeira, words grew quieter, sentences more muffled, and at nightfall the voices ceased altogether.

The maid brought in the gentle lamps. Set down in the places they had occupied for forty years they immediately and faithfully poured into the comfortable study their patterns of light and shade which Dodin's eyes greeted with delighted recognition as the customary and well-regulated lighting of his life's décor. They underlined the grave and prosperous intimacy of the old family house, sending their message of warmth and safety far out into the mystery of the treacherous night.

Then Dodin-Bouffant, as if concluding aloud a lengthy discussion with himself, said: 'There is no doubt about it: the

cuisine of a people is the only accurate witness to its civilization.'
And the divine, subtle, light, graceful and delicious hints of what
Adèle was simmering, occasionally whispering through an open
kitchen door, conferred upon his positive axiom an especial
authority.

When Dodin heard the sound of china, and concluded that the
table was being laid, he excused himself to his disciples:

'I cannot keep you to supper, dear friends. After that infernal
Germany, that long voyage, Adèle and I are somewhat weary.
. . . But we shall resume our customary Tuesdays. . . .'

In fact, he felt an imperious need to savour alone with his
wife the sweetness of everything that was restored to him, and
to concentrate severely, having nearly lost them for ever, upon
the glorious moments his diligent spouse was preparing for him.

The announcement that supper was served seemed suddenly
to tauten and smooth his sagging flesh. He took leave of his
friends and settled down opposite Adèle in one of those famous
armchairs. The good woman, radiant and magnificently rejuvenated, displayed the most reassuring expression on her
round face. Before their Calvary, whenever she had achieved a
masterpiece her nose would turn up and defy all the world's
cooks, or her eyes light up with an intermittent flickering, like
alternating lighthouse beams, or again her mouth would disappear between puffed-out lips. This evening all these signs of joy
spread over her features, and Dodin read into them the happiest
of auguries.

He could not help briefly evoking the watery cabbages, the
sour cream, the infamous hash-balls of Teutonic soups as he
raised to his greedy lips a spoonful of exquisite broth skilfully
married to a cream of lettuce and green beans. And a honeyed
Marétel of the best year dismissed by its scent an atrocious

157

regurgitation of heavy beers. The calf's kidney lay in its handsome rotundity and transparent fat upon a grand bed of fried bread, under the sacred veil of a smooth sauce of simple and yet variegated scents, like the colours of a rainbow. He lifted up his soul to the twin gods of the hearth and of French cookery.

But when he came to the tart of golden Bresse chicken-livers in shrimp gravy, he jumped for joy: life, that is to say the delight of enjoying knowledgeably and to the full the glory of nature developed by man's genius, the security of the next day's meal, and that of the following day, and for ever, the comfortable, broad, placid rapture of his blessed province—life, in short, flowed back into him in all its glory. The anxiety in his eyes dimmed and became that ironical certainty, that happy serenity which had so long shone from him upon the world, and which he had but now recovered. His shoulders to which misfortune had given a slight stoop, straightened up, freed and triumphant. And the Burgundy flowed between his lips like a tide of ambrosia. For a long time he looked at his wife opposite him, who, giving the lie to the false legend that a cook never eats the food she has prepared, was engaged in tracking down in the very bottom of the dish, with a vigorous piece of bread, the tiniest scraps of liver and sauce, genuinely rejoicing in the final traces of her masterpiece. He folded her in a gaze of love and gratitude.

'Adèle,' he said, putting down his napkin, and rising.

She raised her kindly eyes, once more calm and clear, but in which her genius still shone.

'Adèle,' he continued, 'in just a few hours you have succeeded in erasing the very memory of long and cruel trials. We have learned by bitter experience that there is no crisis, no illness, even no death that can equal in suffering and horror the weeks imposed upon us by those sawbones, those abominable "cures" which leave you weak, sick and breathless. Whatever may lie in store for us, we are henceforth fully enlightened upon the worthless deceit of diets. Let us again take up, and never abandon, our good life and our good cookery of the past, and whether in peace or in suffering, whichever it may please God to send us, end our existence in the cult of good fare and household joys.'

He rose to his full height, and leaning across the table took both Adèle's hands in his own, as if asking her to join him in his vow over the memory of the marvellous chicken-liver tart and the noble empty bottles.

Apologia

I hesitated for a long time, at the end of the war, before completing and publishing this book begun on the eve of the catastrophe. Some people will certainly reproach me, perhaps rightly, for what they will call gastronomic futilities when such grave preoccupations obsess men who are barely convalescent, and will wither me for discussing a turbot sauce when the Barbarians are more than ever at the gates of Rome.

However, I made up my mind to do it, and now add to the apparent impropriety of inviting my readers into the kitchen when they should be perorating in the Forum, the audacity of pleading 'not guilty'. I could borrow the elements of my defence from the accustomed thoughts of Dodin-Bouffant himself, and from certain immortal aphorisms of the august shade whose earthly name I write at the head of these pages. If, like the man whose saintly existence I evoke in these chapters and like myself, one admits that cookery is the art of taste as painting is the art of sight and music that of hearing, is not this the time and place to glorify these arts, the spontaneous creations of human fantasy and sensibility in which, in the final analysis, we may perhaps tomorrow be obliged to seek the rules and foundations of the new morality, if reason persists in denying them to us? This argument, on the other hand, is sure to be attacked. *Cuisine* is still the victim of low and deplorable prejudice. Its most noble geniuses have not yet conquered their rights to sit between Raphael and Beethoven, and before some modest learning could be recognized in this humble collection of stories, we should have had to write a fat book to maintain in theses, antitheses and syntheses the view that the gastronomic art, like all other arts, comprises a philosophy, a psychology and an ethic, that it is an integral part of universal thought, that it is bound to the civilization of our earth, to the cultivation of our taste, and thereby to the superior essence of humanity.

I have always thought that art was the effort of genius to find and to express the absolute and profound harmony concealed under the apparent disorder and chaos of nature. I have not forged this definition especially for my hero's dominant passion. But how well it fits! Spread out haphazardly upon a large table all the animal and vegetable products of soil, sky and wave—and reflect upon the intellectual effort, the genial intuition, which will harmonize them, measure them, wrench from their rough outer covering and their dead flesh all their flavours, balance their values, and extract from them all the raptures which nature enclosed in them and which would sleep within them for ever, unknown and useless, if human brains and taste did not compel them to yield up their savoury secrets.

But I shall stop at this brief sketch of a philosophy of transcendental cookery.

Another reason prompted my decision. At this time when France, whose liberty was only rescued at the price of deep scars, facing the future adds up the glories of her past and, so to speak, takes an inventory of her treasures before the task of tomorrow, it seems to me that it cannot be harmful to her destinies to speak with love and conviction of a work in which she has always surpassed other nations.

Great, noble cookery is a tradition of this country. It is an age-old and appreciable element of her charm, a reflection of her soul. To bowdlerize and simplify a great thought of Brillat-Savarin, one can affirm that everywhere else people feed; in France alone do they know how to eat. In France, they have always known how to eat, as they have known how to build incomparable castles, cast unequalled bronzes, make inimitable furniture, create styles subsequently pillaged by the whole world, and invent fashions to make women of all latitudes dream —because, in short, they have taste.

Light, delicate, learned and noble, harmonious and precise, clear and logical, the cuisine of France is linked, by mysterious relationships, with the genius of her greatest men. There is not such a distance as one thinks between, for instance, a tragedy by Racine and a meal conceived by the competent and marvellous host that was Talleyrand, to cite but one single gastronome. The sense of order, the purity of pleasure, the dignity of sensation and the love of line are of the same breed in the poet and the gourmet. If mortadella, which is certainly not to be despised, is close to Goldoni; if the pink jellies with *Rehbraten* in thick yellowish sauce, or the Black Forest meatballs are heavy, thick and massive like German thought, art and literature; there are in a *quiche lorraine*, or Périgord liver, or Savoyard jugged hare, or Dauphinois *gratin*, all the refined riches of France, all her wit, all her gaiety of the bad days as well as the good, all the gravity, too, hiding behind her charms, all her taste for intimate freedom, all her sly wit and her level-headedness, all her love of saving and of comfort, all her substantial strength, all the soul of her fat, fruitful and well-worked soil of which the suave cream, the snowy fowls, the delicate vegetables, the juicy fruits, the splendid cattle and the frank, supple and vigorous wines are the blessed manifestations.

French cuisine sprang from the old Gallo-Latin soil; it is the smile of its lavish countryside. France would no longer be France on the day when one ate there as in Chicago or Leipzig, or drank there as in London or Berlin. A taste for gastronomy is innate in the race. There one cannot, one does not know how to, treat lightly the august task of cooking. I shall remember all my life how, in 1916, on the Champagne front, in bombarded Rheims, in threatened Fismes, in half-destroyed Soissons, I was served lavish meals such as I have never eaten in full peace-time either in New York, Vienna or Constantinople.

Steeped in these beliefs, have I then committed a crime in attempting (surrounded by soldiers covered in glory and noble deeds, by diplomats and ministers burdened with the weighty duty of reconstructing a world, by popular leaders anxious to wrench justice from those who withhold wealth) to portray in these few pages, the figure—old-fashioned, perhaps, but certainly impassioned—of this retired magistrate, a compatriot of the illustrious author of *La Physiologie du Goût*, who from the depths of his Jurassic province, devoted his life and love to one of the oldest and most essential traditions of his country? Dodin-Bouffant is a gourmet as Claude Lorrain is a painter, as Berlioz is a musician. He is of medium height and powerfully built; stout with dignity and with elegance. He is clean-shaven and nearly white of hair—he wears mutton-chop whiskers. He speaks without haste, closes his eyes when in thought, emits aphorisms without pedantry, likes to tease, and does not shrink from broad humour. With the dessert, he enjoys sharing his youthful memories with well-chosen friends, and that is his only reason for preferring Burgundy to Bordeaux. He lives at peace with his inheritance. He is a sage, and a Frenchman of the old school.

A Glossary

OF DISHES, SAUCES AND GARNISHES
MENTIONED IN THE TEXT

(*Translator's note.*—This glossary does not pretend to convey more than a general notion of the type of dish or sauce in question. The recipes involved would fill a large volume, and readers seeking detailed information will themselves be gastronomes and know where to find it. However, many of the *plats* named are not given in modern books on cookery, and some are extremely hard to track down even in the great classics of French cuisine (many of which I have consulted). There are, in fact, a few which I have been quite unable to trace in the short time before going to press—for this I must apologize to the reader. I should also like to remind him that a possible discrepancy between a description in this glossary and a recipe he may have to hand is not necessarily due to error, but to the diverging opinions of many culinary authorities on the proper recipe for a dish. I have simply tried to select the version Dodin would be most likely to have preferred. For good advice on the best sources to consult in compiling this glossary, I am most grateful to Mrs Elizabeth David who, if anyone does, knows all about it. I should also like to thank M. and Madame Lheureux of Nîmes and M. Chabert of Tain-l'Ermitage who have gallantly tried to fill most of my gaps.)

Aïolis: Garlic mayonnaises of various types, often including vegetables, meats or fish. In the singular garlic sauce.

Andouilles: Pork sausage-casing containing meat or tripe from the same animal. For fish sheep-casings are used, and for *andouillettes* beef-casings.

Aspic de Tête de Veau à la Vieux-Lyon: A dish of calf's head in jelly, the aspic highly seasoned and containing wine.

Barigoule, à la: Whole medium-sized potatoes cooked in olive-oil. Another version is with a tomato, garlic and mushroom stuffing braised with bacon in white wine.

Bavaroise au chocolat: A hot frothy drink made of eggs, milk, syrup, rum or kirsch, and chocolate.

Belle Aurore, à la: Generally applies to white or cream sauces coloured and flavoured with tomato purée.

Blanc-Manger, Beignets de: Fritters of an almond cream paste.

Bordelaise (*a*) a mixture of shallots, beef-marrow and parsley pressed on to an *entrecôte* before grilling,

(*b*) a red wine sauce containing shallots, bay, thyme, pepper and mignonette with added butter and cubes of beef-marrow.

Bressane, oeufs à la: Moulds decorated with truffles and whites of hard-boiled eggs, served on artichoke bottoms and coated with Velouté sauce.

Cardinale, Compote de Poires à la: Pears poached in a vanilla syrup and served with a kirsch-flavoured raspberry purée and splintered almonds.

Canard à la Nivernaise: Duck with a garnish of carrots and onions. (See also sauce Nivernaise.)

Célestine, Omelette à la: Two omelettes, one inside the other, each with a different sweet stuffing and glazed in the oven.

Daube, Dindons à la: Boned breast of turkey stuffed with sausage-meat, bacon and truffles soaked in brandy, garnished with ox-tongue, cooked in stock in a terrine and served cold.

165

Daube de Poussins aux Morilles Noires: Baby-chickens braised with white wine and eau de vie with black morel mushrooms in a sealed terrine.

Dauphine, à la: Garnished with rissoled potatoes.

Demidoff, Macaronis à la: Macaroni with a sauce of carrots, celery, turnips cooked in butter, to which truffles are finally added—served *en cocotte.*

Dubarry, à la: Accompanied by cauliflower with Béchamel sauce.

Escargots à la Provençale: Snails prepared in the usual manner and served with garlic-butter and chopped parsley.

Fricassée: Sauté chicken, the sauce bound with egg yolk.

Favorite, Poulet à la: Chicken stuffed with a savoury rice, then poached and served with sauce *suprême* and a garnish of cocks' combs, kidneys and truffles. Foie gras in stuffing.

Fricandeau: Meat or fish, larded, braised and very tender— characteristically can be eaten with a spoon—usually glazed.

Flamand, Potage: Cream of onion and potato soup with cream added.

Gaillarde, Sauce: A Limousin-Marché speciality with *moutarde violette de Brive.*

Grenadin de Poularde: A chicken variety of small, glazed, hot or cold *fricandeau, see* above.

Grand Veneur, sauce à la: A thick game stock and vegetable gravy highly seasoned, with red currant jelly and cream.

Impératrice, Salade à l': A mixture of sliced truffles and arti-choke bottoms dressed with oil and lemon juice.

Lorraine, Salade à la: Either hard-boiled eggs with *fines herbes* and *vinaigrette* or mainly green salad with bacon ribbons and a garnish of mixed raw vegetables.

Maréchale, Truffes à la: Truffle portions egged-and-bread-crumbed then quickly fried in deep fat, probably with asparagus-tips as garnish; calf's brains sometimes added.

Marengo, Poulet: Chicken sauté in oil, with a sauce containing white wine, tomato puree, garlic and mushrooms, served with truffles and fried eggs, *croûtons* and crayfish.

Marceau, St., Potage à la: Pea-soup with finely shredded leeks, chervil and butter.

Ménéhould, Ste, à la: A method of preparing which consists of first braising, then grilling or frying the meat after coating in egg and breadcrumbs.

Mitonnage, bouillon de: Broth in which bread is cooked.

Mirepoix, sauce à la: A basic sauce of vegetables (onions, carrots, turnips, celery, etc.) fried gently in butter, then pulped and used as a basis for braises or sauces.

Mouillette, oeufs à la: Boiled eggs into which 'mouillettes' or small pieces of bread are dipped.

Nichon, à la (oeufs): Two fried eggs side by side.

Nivernaise, sauce: A sauce of dry white wine with shallots, lemon-juice, butter, garlic herbs and egg yolks.

Ouille (also Oille): A ragoût or a soup, an 'olla podrida'.

Pâté Royal: A rich *pâté* in which several kinds of game and domestic meat are combined.

Panade de Blancs de Poularde: A bread-thickened sauce of stock with fillets of chicken-breasts.

Papillote, en: 'In curl-papers', i.e. greased paper.

Persillé: A type of cheese sprinkled with chopped parsley.

Piquante, Sauce: A vinegar and white wine sauce with shallots, gherkins, capers, chervil, tarragon and parsley.

Poupetin de Brochet Fourré: Stuffed pike, boned and stitched and cooked whole.

Prince de Galles, Salade à la: A mixture of lettuce, chervil, watercress, capers, sardines, pimentos: a really pungent salad.

Quenelles: Meat or fish dumplings, in which a cream and egg mixture is incorporated—poached gently. Generally of pike.

Quiches: Savoury tarts with cream, egg and bacon filling.

Ratafia: A liqueur flavoured with bitter kernels of peaches, etc.

Reine, Coulis à la: A sauce of chicken broth thickened with the pounded chicken-meat.

Relevés: Dishes 'relieving', or taking over from the soups as opposed to *entrées.*

Rôties: Hot buttered grilled toast under roasts, or served for tea.

Ramequins: Puff pastry with milk, eggs, cheese.

Rouennaise, Sauce: Bordelaise with raw minced duck livers.

Saingaraz, sauce à la: A julienne (thin slivers) of truffles, tongue, and mushrooms in a Sauce Madère.

Tourte: In some cases an open tart in others a closed pie (as in the case of Dodin's stuffed duckling pie).

Tourterelles, Poupetin de: Boned, stuffed turtledoves, stitched up and cooked whole.

Terrine de Bécasses: Potted woodcock.

Vacherin: An elaborate dessert of ice-cream, crystallized fruit, meringue and whipped cream.

Veau de Rivière: Veal from animals grazed in the water-meadows of the Seine in the Rouen region.

Printed in the United States
by Baker & Taylor Publisher Services